Night Hawks

NIGHT HAWKS

MICHAEL LOYD GRAY

Stories from this novella first appeared, in earlier forms, in the following literary journals: "The Last Train to Chicago" in *the Vincent Brothers Review*; "Just Go to Jesus, Girl" in *Taj Mahal Review*

ISBN 979-8-9908030-8-4 (paperback)
ISBN 979-8-9908030-9-1 (ebook)

Published by Type Eighteen Books
www.typeeighteenbooks.com

I dedicate Night Hawks to my late mother, Dorothy Gray.
She'd have been tickled to see my growth as a writer.

Table of Contents

The Last Train to Chicago

I'm just back from the dumpster, the Chicago train's horn blaring its warning, as Hundley waltzes in with his load on and orders the Blue Plate Special. It's getting late and we stay close at ten now, because there's not enough traffic. The Blue Plate is all we've got left, a mishmash of creamed corn or potatoes. Sometimes fries if there's any in the fryer that haven't drowned in oil.

He's not picky, Hundley. What drunk is? He stops by to soak up the alcohol with whatever we put in front of him. And of course, to chat up Lois, a waitress pushing fifty willing to work late because she needs the money. She's eager to beat feet out of this burg. She has Chicago desires, and her ears prick up every time the train horn whines and calls out to her.

Hundley's been working on her for a few weeks now and I'd venture to guess she's leaning toward it. Bending like a sapling in a stiff wind. I know what goes on in my diner. I catch her glances at him, how she lingers when he gives her a lopsided grin. She fusses over him, and I tell her to be careful what you wish for, darlin', but she laughs, tosses her head back, and says it's only horseplay.

But I know where all that horseplay can end up—hard feelings and broken hearts. Unhappiness and disillusionment. There are a few country songs about all that on the jukebox. Sometimes I play one when Hundley saunters in all cockeyed, and Lois will give me her old evil eye, arms crossed over her chest.

Tonight there's a few fries left that haven't hardened like stones, and Lois fetches a ketchup bottle so Hundley can drown them some more. She touches his shoulder lightly and slides the bottle in front of him. He slaps the bottom of the bottle too hard, and ketchup sprays the plate and counter.

"Whoops-a-daisy," he says, grinning.

"That's okay—no harm done, honey," Lois says, quick to pull a rag from her uniform pocket to mop the counter. She grabs a new ketchup bottle from a booth, gives it a good shake to loosen it up, and sets it next to Hundley's plate.

"Where would you be without her?" he says to me.

"Well, now, I don't rightly know, Hundley. Give me a minute to think on it."

Lois shoots me the evil eye.

"He don't know a gem when he sees it," she says, again touching Hundley's shoulder, and then his elbow, too, but Hundley's too drunk to pick up on it. He shovels the food in and then wipes his mouth. After a sigh, he places his elbows on the counter.

"How about some pie, honey?" Lois says. "Or some cobbler?"

"Do you still have some of that chocolate pie?" Hundley says, eager like a kid.

"We sure do, honey," she says. "And Cool-Whip, too."

"I like me some Cool-Whip just fine," he says, nodding eagerly.

"Well, then you're in luck."

"Don't I know it." He winks at her and pats his belly. "I reckon I've got enough room for some of your pie, Lois."

He makes it sound a little dirty, of course, and Lois blushes slightly, again touching his shoulder, all touchy-feely. Hundley winks at me and I give him a look and go to the kitchen.

While I wash dishes, I hear Hundley laugh and I glance out the little window on the kitchen door: Lois has roosted on a stool next to his, and he has a meaty paw on her knee. She smiles and lets it linger long enough to send the message, and then she brushes it away, delicately. Her raven black hair is a startling contrast to Hundley's thatch of blond curls. She whispers in his ear. He laughs again as she makes her way to the kitchen.

"No good will come of it," I say as she washes her hands.

"Mind your own business, Hank Spencer." She dries her hands on a towel, and I get the old evil eye again.

I dry a dish and plop it into a rack. "What goes on in my diner *is* my business."

"I'm off the clock now."

"But not off the hook."

"You're not my daddy," she says, tapping her foot.

"I should say not. I'm only a couple years older than you."

"*Five* years older," she says. "And you're taking that tone."

"And what tone is *that*?"

"That daddy tone. Like you know what's best."

"Well, I know what's *right*."

"Do you?"

"I like to think so, anyway."

She rummages through her pockets for a cigarette, but she's all out. I give her one of mine and light it.

She exhales the blue smoke slowly, a cloud between us, lingering. "Hundley's going to walk me home," she finally says.

"Uh-huh. I see."

"Do you, Hank?"

"He drinks too much."

"Don't we all?" She attempts to smile but doesn't manage it. She exhales more smoke and looks at her shoes. "What else is there to do in this town?"

"Fair enough, I suppose."

She takes a long pull on the cigarette, its tip glowing red, and exhales. "That's not all. I need a couple days. Clara can fill in okay, but I want those days. I've worked hard for them."

"I never said you didn't. You do work hard."

Her eyes narrow.

"Damn right I do."

"You're the best waitress I've ever had."

"For what that's worth."

"Honest work is nothing to sneer at."

"Maybe."

"No maybes about it."

"Listen," she says. "Hundley and I are going to Chicago. Tonight. We're taking the last train, the midnight one."

"I see."

"So now you know."

I glance at my watch and see it's ten. "Now I know."

"We'll swing by my place and get what I need," she says. "Sorry for the short notice."

I know I should keep my mouth shut, but I can't. "Be sure about things and not *sorry* later. That's all I'm saying."

"There's that tone again, Hank Spencer."

"Sorry. You're a big girl."

"Yeah, I am. And I'm a grown woman."

"Yes, you are."

"And making grown woman decisions," she adds firmly.

I pull a few cigarettes from my pack and give them to her. "For the road. Until you can get more."

"Hundley has money," she says abruptly, too loudly.

"He does okay in that department, I know."

"He'll sleep it off on the train, and then we'll have a fine time down there," she says. "In Chicago."

"That toddlin' town."

"I don't know what that means."

"Never mind."

She's tapping her foot again. I think she's already worried about how it will go, but she's also past the point of no return. She's going. If not for anything else, to see what it might take to stay there. I reach into the bag holding the evening take and give her some bills, more than she has coming for pay.

"Call it an advance. For when you get back. Or if you need another ticket."

She looks up at me. "Hundley's got that covered."

"You never know about things. That's all I'm saying."

"Of course," she says, looking at the bills before slipping them into a pocket. She can't look me in the eye.

"Go on, now, Lois. Go have a fine time of it in the windy city."

"The windy city," she says, nodding. "I've never seen it."

"Well, now you will. You'll see it all."

I'm thinking she may see more than she cares to, but that's on her now. There's no stopping her. It's not my place to do so. I said my piece.

She goes out the door, head down, and then she and Hundley, arm in arm, plunge into the summer night. I watch them from the window until they reach the corner, where they pause for a moment under a streetlight with a cloud of moths batting against the glass, and then they disappear.

I lock the front door behind me and fetch an Old Milwaukee from the cooler. I sit at the counter of my diner and sip beer and look at my watch. There's still time to call Clara and let her know I've got full-time work. Soon, a burst of motivation has me mopping the floors, dusting, and arranging silverware. I put chairs and tables in proper order. I wipe down the long counter and then I'm exhausted. I drink a second Old Milwaukee, sitting at a table with a view of the darkened street. The town has gone to bed.

Soon I hear the horn from the last train to Chicago.

Girl in a Window

She always sits alone, the girl in the window, an elbow resting on the sill. I see her when I take my evening hike, which is more of an odyssey than exercise. It's summer—darkness not creeping in until nine to shroud wounds and secrets—and that's when I first see her in the half-light, a shadow girl.

On this night, I am back from far out in the countryside, from out deep into farm country and then timber lands, a satisfactory burn in my legs, endorphins raging, my mind mostly purged of Afghanistan—for this evening, anyway—and I linger on the street, across from the girl in the window. I'm on the way back to the rooms above the diner Hank Spencer lets me use. I sip from the water bottle and then, impulsively, raise it in salute. She does not move. Not an inch. If she notices me, she must simply not care. The shadow remains in the shadows.

I sometimes wonder, *after* a long hike, when my exhausted body has worn my mind into a groove of dim clarity, if she's merely a mannequin stationed there as some kind of joke. Long hair flows across her shoulders, and that's all I can see of this wraith, this girl phantom who occupies a window as if she were a shadowy painting, with the window as the frame. I can't see her face—not the details, the contours. They are shrouded by the half-light, and by the cascading hair, long bangs falling into her eyes and tickling her cheeks.

Night is when I must walk. Hike. Do some recon. Often for hours, for miles. Out in the timber lands past the soybean and corn fields surrounding the town, where it seems like shadows dance around every tree, until aching feet and heavy thighs signal the brain to relent, to be okay with a little darkness—and then back I go, the girl in a window still framed, still motionless.

Night is when walls can close in, and I walk to tire myself until I can endure confinement and accept my bed. I walk in the night to make my muscles ache and my mind cool down, thoughts mostly dispersing to the edges of consciousness, but always there, lingering and lurking, still potent but at bay for a time, and then I can submit to the fitful sleep and survive until morning light trickles through my own window and warms my face.

During the day, there is no girl. The window is just a window and not a frame. Everything is different during the day—clearer, safer. Light helps discourage dark thoughts from settling in like clouds that refuse to leave. At night, my small rooms become cloudy and oppressive. Night is an ordeal, boiled down to a manageable level only after hiking toward no goal but to wear down and survive blackness until light can sort things out. Barely. During the day, I walk by the girl's window and stop but see nothing. It's only an apartment building two blocks down from where I live, in two rooms above Hank Spencer's diner.

I don't need to hike during daylight. But I drift around town anyway, leisurely, taking many breaks. I might walk across the railroad tracks to the park and sit at a picnic table with a couple Old Milwaukees and a ham and cheese from the diner, admiring dozens of initials carved into the table. So many romances over many years. In the afternoons, I might eat again or rest on my bunk. Sometimes, I read a book or magazine, to distract my mind.

In my bunk, waiting for the sun to go down, I think of all those carved initials—who they must represent and what happened to them. I come up with names for the initials. I conjure up all sorts of combinations.

Once I saw "HK" and wondered if it was Hank Spencer who carved them. He's a good man and has been generous. Gave me a place to stay— until I get on my feet, he says. Hank was in the first Gulf War. We're brothers in arms and all that shit. He knows the drill.

But he came home from his war to inherit a diner. It gives him purpose, I suppose. A life worth living. He says he had a wife, Thelma, but she ran off. Caught a train to Chicago and vanished, like my own pa did. Shit happens, I tell Hank, and he grins and nods. Yeah, he knows the drill all right.

Sometimes I think about girls, sure. But I don't know any girls. There's Lois, a waitress at the diner. She's not bad-looking—a curvy butt and good legs, but she's too old for me. It'd be like dating an aunt. The sex—I don't know how that would go. I've never been with an older woman.

Truth be told, Lois did give me the eye a few times. Then *she* disappeared, too. It's like there's an invisible tractor beam—like in the old Star Trek movies I watched in Crapghanistan—that comes down and snatches folks straight up out of this burg. Sometimes at night, deep out in the timber lands, I look up at a star-filled sky for that tractor beam, but it's not interested in me.

The girls I knew from high school mostly fled to Chicago or elsewhere after graduation. Nothing much for them around here, I reckon, but marriage to some sodbuster farmer or a dickhead working at the grain elevator. I lost touch with my high school friends when I joined the Army. I didn't have all that many to start with.

My father disappeared many years ago, up and left one night after a second helping of tuna casserole. I did think it odd at the time that he walked out with a six-pack of Budweiser under his arm. My mother is out at the county nursing home and doesn't know me anymore. Shit happens.

Now here I am, trying to walk Crapghanistan off, I reckon, and unsure how that's going. Good days and bad days, but plenty of exercise. I'm in decent physical shape, anyway. And eager for something. A job, eventually, if I can find something I won't hate, something with decent pay. Maybe in the building trades, working with my hands. Honest, hard work with minimal thinking involved. One day, I was helping Hank put up some new cabinets in the kitchen. I'm not a half-bad carpenter and maybe that's where I'm headed. I've seen enough torn down. Building something might be good.

When we finished installing the cabinets, I felt good about the work, what we accomplished, how it looked and all, and suddenly, I wanted to talk a little. I told Hank about the girl in the window and how I could never quite make her out.

"Where's this?" he asked as he opened and closed a cabinet.

"Down the street. Two blocks, on the other side—that old apartment building."

Hank's jaw went slack in that same way a team leader might have looked at me when he clearly believed I'd fucked up somehow and needed the old, Come-to-Jesus talk.

"Next to the drugstore?"

"That's the one. First floor."

He placed hands on hips and stared at the floor. I've seen that look before, too. "Nobody lives there," he said eventually. "That building's condemned. It's going to come down soon."

"I see."

"Do you?"

I couldn't make words come together. "I don't know what to say, Hank."

He sighed, the kind of sigh that oozed out slowly at the end of a long day. "Well, it was probably some kids playing around in there," Hank said.

"Yeah," I said. "Maybe so."

That night, when I'd come back from hiking out in the timber lands, I passed by the apartment house but didn't see anybody in the window. I waited a while, but nothing happened. I didn't know what to make of that.

I sat on the edge of my bunk much of the night. I tried reading, but it didn't help. I attempted to recall the girl in the window, but her image had faded into a sort of dull, gray mass. Finally, I got a few hours of sleep and then in the early morning hours, I sat up in my bunk, staring at the ceiling, until I heard Hank stirring downstairs.

I showered, packed a bag, and went downstairs. Hank gave me money for a train ticket and walked me to the station. He's like that, always helping folks out. We talked about the weather for a little while, and how a storm might be coming but the crops needed the rain. Then he waited patiently as I got on the train.

I was down at the VA in Chicago for a few days. I saw one of the shrinks several times. He said I'll probably be okay. Time will tell. Be patient, he said. Get some sleep.

At the VA, it's all about waiting in lines and at the end of the day, you take some pills. They have pills of all colors. Pills for this and that and everything in between. They upped my dosage. Somebody said that ought to do it. Somebody else said, you're adjusting. Give it time.

Time's what I got, I reckon. Time and pills.

But I didn't tell them about the girl in the window.

Just Go to Jesus, Girl

Clara knew when it came down to it, she wouldn't say who'd knocked her up. There was still time before crossing that bridge. She wasn't showing yet and still worked full shifts at the diner filling in for Lois, who'd apparently run off to big city dreams.

But there was talk that Lois would return from Chicago, and Clara would go back to part-time, which would really cut into her tips. She needed the money because the baby's daddy didn't appear to be the type to step up. He was more likely to vanish.

Clara would work as much as she could before her baby bump was obvious. She didn't think she could stomach the glares as she waddled from table to table, feeling eyes on her and imagining the harsh judgments behind them. Hank said he wouldn't be surprised to see Lois walk in any day now, and maybe that would be for the best.

Lois was Clara's only friend, although they were more than twenty years apart in age. Each day Lois stayed away was dollars in Clara's pocket, but she also missed Lois and wished she'd come home anyway. She didn't think anyone but Lois would understand her predicament.

Every morning before heading to the diner, Clara would look at her figure in the mirror. It was like waiting for a doorbell to ring, announcing the unwanted guest. As it was, she was good at coaxing good tip money. She understood men and the ways they liked to be flattered—well, except for her baby's father. She'd heard he'd already bolted for Milwaukee. Classy.

So that was that.

Clara's blonde hair danced on her shoulders, and sometimes she wore it in a ponytail that swished back and forth. She was twenty-two but could pass for seventeen. One night, a trucker called her "Babyface," and during a short lull after dinner hour, she cried in the ladies' room.

Once the bump arrived, she wouldn't be a babyface anymore. Other words would apply.

No, there was no white knight coming to save her. She was on her own. Her folks were self-righteous Bible thumpers and never missed a Sunday at Community Baptist Church. They wouldn't understand, *couldn't* understand such a thing. It violated their narrow view on righteous living. If they knew about the baby, they'd demand that she repent. Her mother would wag a finger in her face and utter her favorite phrase: "Just go to Jesus, girl. Ask forgiveness and seek redemption."

Clara didn't think she needed to be forgiven or redeemed, but she certainly felt bad about it all. The bump was inconvenient, an accident—a mistake made when she hadn't said no the one time it really counted. She didn't think it made her a bad person. Just an unlucky one.

Now the bill was coming due. She felt trapped.

When she came out of the ladies' room one afternoon, Hank looked concerned. She knew he was a decent man with a good heart, a fair boss. He was patient, even keeled. But she'd been in there for a while. A second, smaller rush of patrons would filter in soon. The nightcrawlers, Hank called them.

She sucked in a few breaths and let them out slowly. The room's lights seemed brighter. Hank stopped counting the money in the till to look up at her, squinting.

"You doing okay, Clara?" he asked.

She nodded and forced a thin smile. "Some indigestion. Good to go."

"You're not sick, are you?"

"No, I'm not sick. I'm fine."

Hank glanced at his watch. "You're sure it's nothing?"

Carefully, she placed napkins into the holder on the nearest table. "There's nothing wrong with me."

"Okay, okay—I'm only checking."

"I needed to get my second wind. You know—for the nightcrawlers."

"They'll crawl through the door any time now," he said, and at that moment, a trio of smiling, boisterous truckers walked in, the little bell on the door ringing abruptly.

Clara pulled her shoulders back. The truckers seemed to have already tossed down a few beers. She could expect some clumsy come-ons and coarse language. She was used to that. Still, there were good tips to be made.

"Well, here we go," Hank said. "No rest for the wicked, I reckon."

"Who's wicked?" she said.

He looked up, his eyebrows tilting together. "Nobody. It's just a saying."

"Okay," she said. "I suppose."

Hank handed over a stack of menus. "Are you sure you're doing okay? You seem off your game some." He touched her elbow lightly, but she pulled away. She regretted it, knew he didn't mean anything by it. She'd probably get the same over at the truckers' table. She steeled herself.

"Yes, I'm sure I'm okay. But thanks for asking."

"You look a little flushed."

"It's nothing," she said, grabbing a pitcher of water. "Off to the races. Here we go."

"Well, it's a marathon and not a sprint," Hank said. "Everything's some sort of race, I suppose."

She let that sink in, self-consciously feeling her stomach, but it was still smooth. "Don't I know it."

"Know what?"

"The race," she said. "You have a choice—you can run it long or run it short."

He shrugged, and she couldn't put it off any longer. The truckers were antsy. She went over and pretended to care. She knew how to flip the switch. The truckers ordered the Blue Plate Special—ham slathered in thick chicken gravy, and two sides—creamed corn swimming in melted butter and lima beans.

When she brought them beers, they cheered and called her "darlin'," and "honey," and "missy." They clinked the cans together, toasting something she didn't understand. But she wasn't listening to them anymore. It was all noise. She was already in the next race. It was the sprint and not the marathon, and it would be over soon enough.

Wrong Turn

Lois took the last train home from Chicago. She'd finally dumped that prick Hundley back at the sleazy Loop hotel. Hundley had promised a fine time in "Chi-Town." They'd see sights, he said, live it up. Dance and scarf down deep-dish pizza at Lou Malnati's. But Hundley mostly drank, and she drank with him, thinking they'd be on the same wavelength. But there was no dancing and few sights, and she was fed up with deep-dish pizza and the rundown hotel.

Then Hundley put the back of his hand across her face when she told him to tone down the drinking, and that was the last straw.

The porter nodded as Lois picked her way down the steps from the train clutching her bag. Nobody else got off. A single light lit the platform poorly. A moth circled the light madly, and she sympathized with its dilemma. She was dizzy from going in circles, too. The train pulled away slowly, fitfully, the horn blaring. Inside the station a clerk dozed at a counter. He didn't look up. Lois knew him—knew his face, anyway—from waiting on him at Hank's Diner.

She saw there'd been rain. Water pooled in the gutters, making a gurgling sound as it trickled down sewers; everything watered down and slick—cleansed. It struck her how quiet it was compared to Chicago. The stillness was deafening. She heard a symphony of crickets serenading as she crossed the street and walked past the pawn shop—its green neon sign turned off—and the Speedway station, brightly lit although there were no cars at the pumps.

The diner was ahead, darkened. She wondered how well Clara had filled in for her, and whether the same boy was still sniffing around. Mostly, she wondered how many people Hank had told that Lois had been a damned and naïve fool to traipse off to Chicago with that prick

Hundley. Well, she certainly had it coming if he had. She'd made that bed all by herself.

At the corner, she looked down the side street at the back of the diner and saw lights in Hank's apartment. It didn't surprise her. She stopped and stared at the soft white glare, clutching her bag with both hands. What was he doing awake? She knew he sometimes had trouble sleeping. She hoped he didn't drink himself to sleep every night. That was a dead end. She'd tried it until she finally understood it was better to lose sleep than wake up hungover, too.

Lois walked down the street and knocked on Hank's door. A dog barked in the distance. He answered after a moment, but she didn't think he looked all that surprised.

"Well—did you take a wrong turn in Chicago?"

"That's *so* funny, Hank Spencer."

"It's a *little* bit funny."

"I suppose that'll be the new joke."

"Only if you let it."

"It's really up to me?"

"*Everything* is up to you."

"I suppose we'll see about that."

He swung the door wide. "C'mon, now—we're letting flies in."

He took her bag and put it in a corner. She'd never been to his apartment. It was surprisingly neat and smelled fresh. The furniture was nice—a leather sofa, loveseat, and large coffee table. It was a bigger space than she'd imagined, with a large kitchen area at the back.

"Can I have some water, Hank?"

"Coming up."

While he fetched a glass from a cabinet and filled it, she noted that someone was waiting on her for a change, and not the other way around. That prick Hundley had barely lifted a finger to do anything for her. He'd even left her alone in the hotel room a few times while he went off to see friends about "business." On one occasion, a sleazeball with greasy hair stopped by, and they'd huddled together out of earshot. The sleazeball left Hundley a package, and Lois had quickly figured out that his business was shady. She didn't want the details in her head.

Hank handed her the glass and sat in an easy chair across from the sofa, holding a glass of whiskey neat.

"Thanks," she said, gulping. She was thirstier than she'd thought.

Hank sipped the whiskey.

"How many of those have you had, Hank?"

"First one. A nightcap." He held it up in salute.

"Nightcaps can turn into all night," she said.

"If you let them."

"You don't let them?"

"You know the score. You win some, you lose some."

She leaned back against the sofa. "Don't I know it."

"And how *is* old Hundley anyway?"

"Old Hundley is a sonofabitch."

"Clearly."

"Hundley's a gold-plated prick."

The corners of Hank's mouth turned up slightly. "Tell me something I *don't* know."

"He sells drugs. How about that? He picks them up in Chicago."

"Now *that* I didn't know."

"Well, now you do," she said. "How about I have one of those whiskeys, too."

He poured her one and she sipped, feeling it burn on the way down to explode in her stomach. She sagged now into the sofa.

"I surely don't want Hundley and his drugs in the diner," Hank said after a moment.

She looked up at him. "Hundley might not see it that way."

"Well, he's not the decider."

"He thinks he is. Trust me on that."

"Thinking and knowing are two very different things."

"Yeah? So, what's the difference?"

"One's a wish. The other's a fact."

Lois had never heard Hank sound so manly. Decisive. Capable. She'd always wondered how well he could handle himself. He was a veteran, she knew, from one of the gulf wars. He'd seen some action. Awarded a medal, too. But he never talked about that. He was built solid and had all his hair still, with a few flecks of gray at the temples. Not a bad-looking man, really. He'd look sharp in a blazer and a crisp shirt with a collar—quite different from the man in a smock and apron.

"Are you sleeping okay these days?" she asked.

He sipped whiskey, eased back into the chair, and glanced at the ceiling. "You know how it is with late night work. I sleep when I can."

"But now we close at ten. That should make it easier."

He stared at the ceiling. "I reckon I'm still adjusting to getting home a little earlier."

"Everything takes time," she said, tossing down the rest of the whiskey and making a face.

Hank finished his and leaned forward. "Are you coming back to work?"

She picked absently at a button on her blouse. "How did Clara work out?"

He shrugged. "Sometimes she seems distracted."

"Boyfriend troubles."

"I see."

"How about we have another whiskey. Will that break any rule?"

"None I know of," he said. "Do you want ice in yours this time?'

"Is it better with ice?" Her face flushed slightly.

"It's certainly colder."

"I'll try the ice."

He brought the whiskeys, and they silently sipped for a while.

"I could come back to work in a couple days," Lois finally said.

"Sounds about right."

He raised his glass, and they clinked them together.

"I want to get my legs under me again," she said. "I've mostly sat around for a few weeks now."

Hank leaned forward, his shoulders spreading as he leaned his elbows on his knees. "How bad was it in Chicago?"

She looked into her glass. "It wasn't good." Her eyes teared up, and she dabbed them with the back of her hand.

"Can you talk about it?"

She finished the whiskey. Her head was swimming a little. But it dulled the pain, too. "He hit me. That bastard Hundley hit me."

Hank stiffened. He set down his glass roughly. "Damn. Sonofabitch."

"He used the back of his hand and not a fist."

"What are you going to do?"

"What *can* I do? It's his word against mine. No witnesses, no evidence."

Hank got up and went to the window. He stared into the night with his arms crossed tightly over his chest. "I won't let him in the diner. He won't set foot there anymore. That's final."

"What if he does?"

"He'll pay."

She smiled. "Are you a white knight now?"

He turned to her, his frame blocking the scant light from the street. "You should tell the police."

"Nothing would come of that."

"At least they'd know."

"And then it would be all over town." Lois sighed. Her eyes fluttered. "I'm tired. Exhausted."

"Some sleep will even you out," he said.

"But I can't face walking home to those small rooms." She glanced around. "Can I sleep here tonight?"

"Well, sure. Of course you can." He shoved his hands into his pockets.

She watched him fidget. He seemed like a boy on a first date. It was sweet and unexpected.

He walked past her. "I'm going to put fresh sheets on the bed, Lois."

"The sofa is fine," she said. "I can make out okay here."

"I won't hear of it. A guest doesn't sleep on a lumpy sofa."

"So, I'm a guest now?"

They made eye contact and held it. Hank was the first to look away. Her face burned from the whiskey.

"I'll go see about those sheets," he said.

He hesitated for a few seconds and then went to the bedroom. She heard him opening and closing a closet. No doubt tidying up, too. It was all very endearing. He'd always had a boyish charm about him. She'd known him a good ten years and realized she'd never really thought of him having women over and needing to quickly find fresh sheets for the bed.

She smiled as she imagined herself in that bed with him. It didn't seem crazy at all.

Objects in Mirror

Tyler took a laborer job demolishing a building, the one where he'd imagined a girl in a window. He considered Afghanistan to be in his rearview mirror, but like the old safety warning goes: "Objects in mirror are closer than they appear."

His foreman, an ex-Navy SEAL, had a soft spot for vets with strong backs and arms who did what they were told without a lot of pesky questions. It wasn't rocket science, what Tyler was paid to do. It was mindless grunt work. He hauled heavy debris—bricks, concrete blocks, shattered beams, shards of glass—in a wheelbarrow and acted as a gopher when someone needed tools and supplies.

He was low man on the pole, as he'd been when he first arrived in Afghanistan and that was okay, familiar. Expected. That was how it was when you started over and attempted to build yourself back up again, like a snake shedding old skin. The construction work was hard, dusty, and grimy, but it was a paycheck. And an accomplishment. His first since Afghanistan. At the end of each long day, he was exhausted; his muscles ached, and his mind slowed, and that was a blessing. Part of the healing process, he'd been told. He even began to sleep a little better. The night hikes ceased; fear of night eased.

But that first day on the job, before bulldozers with jagged jaws gouged great holes in the building, slowly toppling it into rubble—like shattered buildings he'd seen in Afghanistan—Tyler stared at the apartment window where he thought he'd seen the girl. He'd finally accepted that it had been his imagination playing tricks and nobody had lived there for a long time. The condemned building teetered and the girl with it. She was bulldozed and shredded and atomized like the debris he swept up and hauled out every day.

But he wondered what the girl in the window symbolized. Innocence?

He'd lost that in Afghanistan. Innocence was the first casualty in war. And there had been another girl in Afghanistan, in a village they hiked through while looking for the Taliban. She, too, sat in a window, watching them pass by. She was pretty, with strands of hair streaming from under her hijab. Her blue eyes were luminous, and those eyes had stayed with him, even when he caught the big bird home. He'd waved at her that day, but she didn't wave back. Her gaze remained stoic. He thought he'd seen her in the condemned building's window, and he still wanted her to wave back. Some sort of closure, he supposed.

He talked to a VA shrink who suggested Tyler saw an innocent girl because he wished to reclaim his own lost innocence. Tyler wasn't sure that it was possible, but he nodded a lot when the shrink spoke. It was a pretty theory, but Tyler didn't think of innocence as something someone could find again and refurbish it. The shrink had never been to Afghanistan, had never served anywhere at all. His notion of innocence was an altogether different kind of animal.

On that first early morning on the job, several old salts on the crew caught Tyler staring dumbstruck at the building, and one of them, a bearded, burly man, said, "Bud, are you going to be one of them squirrely vets who shits himself if a car backfires?"

"Or if someone farts?" one of the other men said, and they all laughed.

"Or he sees a mouse, and thinks it's the Taliban," said another.

"Well, now," Tyler said, smiling pleasantly, "get a car and let's put it to the test. I'll let you boys check my pants. But if you fart, check your *own* pants."

The men laughed, and word spread that Tyler could give as good as he got, a valued skill on a crew fueled by so much testosterone. It had been the same in Afghanistan. You were part of a crew with a pecking order, and you had to prove yourself before people stopped crapping on you. Shit rolled downhill. And Tyler hoped that belonging to something again would make Afghanistan fade faster. With each shovelful, with each wheelbarrow load, Tyler believed he symbolically hauled away the past to clear a path toward a future.

Another theory.

But first, the work needed to last. He'd heard from the old salts that once a big job like this one was done, most of the laborers were let go. The lazy ones, the ones who were mouthy and complainers and always found ways to dodge a task or sneak a break, would be the first cuts. Tyler worked hard and completed every task handed him, no matter how hard and menial. Low man on the pole has nowhere to climb but up, he reminded himself. He simply grinned whenever the old salts called him Soldier Boy. Soon enough, they called him Tyler. Rogers, the foreman, came around one day toward the end of the job, during the end of Tyler's lunch break.

"Tyler, I hear tell you can hang cabinets and even make the doors fit right."

"I reckon I've got an eye for it, yes, sir."

"Hank Spencer told me about your work when I saw him at the diner."

"Hank's a good man."

"Yes, he is. If he says you're a carpenter, then you are."

"You want some cabinets hung, Mr. Rogers?"

"This job's over now. But there are more, smaller jobs. I need a good carpenter. Are you up for that?"

"Yes, sir. I'd like to give it a try."

"Ain't no *trying* involved, son. It's all about *doing*."

Mr. Rogers sounded like his team leader in Afghanistan.

"Yeah, I can do it for you. Just put me to work."

"But there's one other issue, my friend. This business about imagining a girl in a window—that's over and done with?"

Tyler sighed. He hoped it was. But that wouldn't be the right answer, the *practical* answer. He went with practicality.

"Yes. I know how it sounds," Tyler said.

"Son, it don't bother me. Okay? It is what it is. I saw some things, too."

"Yes, sir."

"We all bring somebody like that back home. Stowaways."

"You had one, too?"

"I did." He looked away. "But after a while, we must evict them. There's no room for both of you."

Tyler nodded, looking down. He wanted to cry but could not allow it.

Rogers wrote an address on a card and gave it to him. "You know where this is?"

Tyler looked at the card. "Over by the grain silos."

"That's right. Take a couple days off, son—you've earned them. You did fine here. But show up at that address ready to work."

"Yes, sir. I appreciate it. Thank you, sir."

It was a lot of sirs he was tossing around, but he knew he couldn't go wrong that way with Rogers. He was old school. Sir went a long way with his type. Tyler stuffed the card into his pants and gathered his stuff. He nodded at several of the old salts as he headed down the street, toward the diner. They nodded back.

Tyler felt he'd earned a break, and a cold Old Milwaukee sounded good. It was a fine day to drink a couple cold beers while the day shed into night. Night was not to be feared any more. That was the theory, anyway. His hope.

Then he had a burst of confidence. He'd go see what Clara was up to, that pretty blonde who waited tables at the diner. Halfway there, he did finally cry but felt good about it. He sheltered a moment under a low-hanging tree limb and mopped his tears with the backs of his hands. It was a feeling he couldn't really describe—clean, lighter.

Tyler didn't expect to see the innocent girl in the window again. That was certainly the way to look at it, anyway. She'd been torn down and hauled away with all the other debris. He was as sure of it as he could be about anything. He walked a few steps with closed eyes, heading to the diner to speak to the pretty waitress, as the warm sun dried his tears.

The Off Ramp to Nowhere

Hank put some extra into Clara's pay. It hadn't been a good night for tips and with Lois coming back in a couple days, Clara would slide back to part-time shifts. He felt sorry for her. She was only a kid. She'd never been anywhere in her life and waiting tables in a greasy spoon was the off-ramp to nowhere.

He fetched an Old Milwaukee from the cooler and sat at a table by a window. It was raining; drops pelted the glass. Clara sat down and nursed a Coke. They were run off their feet and sat a while, watching the rain.

"I need to get me a real job, Hank."

"Don't we all?" He was surprised t.

"But you have this diner," she said.

"It was given to me. I didn't build it up."

"I wish someone would give *me* a diner."

He sipped beer and looked at her angelic face framed by long strands of blonde hair. "What would you do with a diner?"

"For starters, I'd put some plants in here. Some flowers, too. And new pictures."

He looked around. Plants weren't a bad idea. The pictures, too. That was a job he could offer and then slip her a few more bills.

"What about college?" he asked.

"My folks don't have any money."

"There's student loans."

She shrugged. "I don't know what I'd take at college. I barely passed high school." She leaned back in her chair, crossed her arms over her chest, and watched water dripping down the window. The rain had picked up and drummed on the roof. A car turned down the street and its headlights flashed in the window.

"Well, what do you like, Clara?"

She shrugged again.

"Okay," he said. "So, what *interests* you?"

"I don't know." She frowned. "Everybody is supposed to know that, but I don't have a frickin' clue."

"You only have to give it some thought."

"I have. Trust me. But nothing really comes to me."

He finished his beer but decided against another one; it might set a bad example for Clara. He had a feeling she was down about something—more than only her job. He remembered she had a boyfriend.

"So, how's that boyfriend coming along. What does he do?"

"Nothing. He don't do anything. And he flew the coop."

"He's gone?"

"That's right. Milwaukee. Now he can be a deadbeat up there, too, for all I care."

"Sorry," was all Hank could think of saying.

"Don't feel sorry for me."

"That's kind of harsh, isn't it?"

"Says the man who has a diner to keep him going."

"I'm a glorified short-order cook, when you boil it down."

"But you're still the boss of you."

"That's not saying much."

"Well, it beats my deal by a lot."

Thunder cracked, and Clara startled. The rain fell hard, and rivers of it flowed down the glass. They couldn't see outside anymore.

"The streets will flood if this keeps up," Hank said. "The sewers aren't built for this amount of water."

"I'm pregnant," Clara said.

A flash of lightning lit up the diner.

Hank sighed, buying time. He felt queasy.

"You don't look it," he said.

"I am—okay? I'm not making it up."

"But now—"

"No buts about it. I did the test. It was positive. I checked twice." She placed a hand on her belly and left it there.

"Do your folks know?"

"God, no. Do you think I'm insane? They'd hand me a Bible as they tossed me out the door."

He could believe it. He knew her folks. Clara had no chance with them. Thunder cracked again, and as the diner lit up, he could see her face. She was frightened.

"What do I do, Hank? Can you tell me that?"

He stared at her, but words wouldn't come out. When he was married, he and his wife tried to have children, but she had a miscarriage. It was merely bad luck, he knew, but it also felt like she blamed him. Little things angered her. He dropped a glass in the kitchen sink one day and it broke.

"You never fail to disappoint me, Hank," his wife had said.

"It's only a glass. We can buy another one. We can buy a dozen if you like."

But he knew it wasn't about broken glasses. It was the disappointment of living in a small town where nothing much happened, and nothing to give her life more meaning, like a child.

And then one day she walked out and moved to Chicago. She'd said if she couldn't have kids, then she didn't want to be married to a short order cook who came home smelling like every greasy item on the diner menu. That was nearly ten years ago. He didn't think of himself as the one she should ask for help, but he realized he was all Clara had.

"What do you *want* to do about it?" he asked.

For a moment, she let her face fall into her hands. He waited patiently while she sobbed. For now, all he could do was be there. It wasn't a time for words. When she looked up, her face was red and tear stained.

"What a fucking mess," she said.

More thunder cracked.

"Maybe I should go out in that storm and let lightning strike me dead."

"But if you did, who'd wait tables until Lois is back?"

Clara stared at him, a grin spreading slowly across her face. She nodded and wiped her eyes.

They sat like that for a long moment. The rain slackened, and bursts of thunder sounded farther away.

"Will the streets really flood?" she asked.

"Yeah, and the water will clog the drains with debris."

"Somebody will have to clear them."

He nodded. "But the sun will eventually come out again. It will all dry out."

"That's a good way to look at it, I suppose."

"Is that how you're looking at it?"

She bit her bottom lip. "I guess so. Things need to be unclogged, and everything will be fine. Right? Simple, really."

After some time, the rain ended, and Hank walked Clara home. He didn't want her to be alone. It was all he could do, but he believed it was enough for the moment. The street she lived on was a series of pools. Water rushed down the storm drains; it made a soothing, continuous sound. Lightning flashed on the horizon, but there was no more thunder. The storm had moved on. They slipped off their shoes and socks and waded across the street.

Little Black Bows

Lois splurged on new work shoes with thick foam soles and extra padding in the heels. They weren't much to look at—pink monstrosities with ludicrous, little black bows on the tongues—but they were on sale dirt cheap, and she didn't figure to stare at those ridiculous little bows while balancing plates and floating table to table like some bee with too many flowers to pollinate.

"These here are pro-fession-al footwear," the oily young clerk at Buster Brown's Shoe Store had said eagerly, winking. "Like walking on a cloud, ma'am."

Lois had winced at the ma'am business—and the creepy wink—but let it go.

"Uh-huh," she'd said. "We'll see about that."

She had slipped them on to take a few steps, and it was like heaven inside those shoes. Floating on clouds indeed. She'd mostly sat around during the recent debacle in Chicago with that prick Hundley, and now she was ramping up to be run off her feet again after a few weeks away.

It was a Friday, a busy shift at the diner, and Hank had kept Clara on for the night, too. Hank's Diner was usually a one-man, one-woman operation, but Lois knew Hank had a soft spot for Clara, who needed money to get away from her parents. Two servers meant competition for tips, but Lois had gotten a few dollars off Hundley before she'd split for Chicago and came home with her tail between her legs.

She felt like an older sister to Clara, who didn't have one, and didn't begrudge the girl a few tips. Clara hadn't gotten many breaks in life. Lois could relate; she'd run off to Chicago thinking it was the start of a new life, but all she got was the back of his hand. Hank took her back on and didn't try to lecture her. He was that way, sometimes generous to a fault but not a great businessman. Still, the diner seemed to make enough to balance it all out, mostly because the good townsfolk didn't have many choices for a meal out.

Lois had slipped into her pink uniform in the ladies' room—she never wore it to work—when Clara popped in with her chirpy bird voice.

"Look at those precious little black bows," Clara said, hands on hips, staring at the new shoes.

Lois applied lipstick and glanced at her in the mirror. Did the bows stand out *that* much? "Noticed them right off, did you, honey?" she asked.

Clara shrugged. "They're hard to miss. They jump out at you."

"They can probably see them from outer space." Lois laughed, smudged her lipstick, and had to start over.

"But the black bows set off the pink nicely," Clara said.

"Really? You think so?"

"Like a cherry on top."

"Uh-huh," Lois said, tilting her head side to side to check each corner of her mouth. "If you say so."

"I do. So, what are they called?"

"Pro-fession-al footwear," Lois said, mimicking the oily clerk from Buster Brown's.

"Well, they look comfy, Lois. Give them that. Sturdy and wide, by the look."

"That's the idea, hun. Otherwise, I wouldn't be caught dead in these. Don't *even* let me be buried in them."

"Now, they're not as bad as all that."

"They're hideous at best. But comfort sometimes trumps fashion, I suppose. It's not like we're models."

Clara looked at herself in the mirror. "I wouldn't mind being a model. That would really be something. But I guess I'm too—big-boned."

Lois frowned. "You're shapely, and there's nothing wrong with that. Some meat on the bone ain't a bad thing. Models are all skin and bones and live on yogurt. Most of them are unhappy. They make themselves throw up."

"My mom says it's our Swedish heritage." Clara turned sideways to assess her silhouette. She rubbed her belly softly. "We're from a long line of big-boned women."

Lois cast a sidelong glance at the girl. "You feeling okay?"

"My stomach's a little upside down. But I'll be okay. I took some TUMS."

"What's got you in such a state? Something you ate?"

"Oh, probably."

"Do you need to sit down for a while, hun?"

"If I sit down, I won't want to get up."

"I hear you on that."

"You know what black bows symbolize?" Clara arranged her bangs in the mirror.

"Poor fashion sense?"

"Love."

Oh, dear," Lois said, checking her mascara one last time. "Let's not even go there. We should leave love here in the ladies' room."

"Chicago didn't go well?"

"Let's say Chicago wasn't as bright as these new shoes."

"I thought you and Hundley were a thing."

"He's a *thing* all right. Live and learn."

"Don't I know it."

Lois noticed Clara's glum look.

"Are you sure you're okay, baby? What about that boyfriend of yours? What's his name, Teddy?"

"Tony." Clara sagged against the counter and sighed heavily.

"Trouble in paradise?" Lois said.

"There never was any paradise that I saw. And now he's gone."

"Gone?"

"As in vanished – poof!"

"Mercy me," Lois said. "Where to?"

"Milwaukee."

She smirked. "Well, look at it this way, hun—you don't need anybody who picks Milwaukee over Chicago."

"You've been to Milwaukee?"

"Once. It ain't Chicago."

"But better than here."

"Most places are," Lois said.

"Maybe I should go to Chicago," Clara said. "What do you think?"

"Be careful what you wish for, hun."

"What does *that* mean?"

Lois looked one last time at her lipstick before turning to Clara.

"Look—the thing about a big town is not so much the town, but how *you* are in it. Understand? Some folks do okay, but some thrive better in a burg like this. I reckon that's *my* lot, anyway."

Clara's eyes widened. "What went wrong down there in Chicago?"

"Hundley went wrong, that's what. He's an asshole. Live and learn, I always say."

She leaned closer to the mirror, checking her cheek for any lingering redness from where Hundley had clocked her, but there was nothing to see.

"What did you learn in Chicago, Lois?"

She narrowed her eyes at the girl. "That little black bows don't always symbolize love. How about that?"

Clara sniffed, almost like she might cry. "But now you have those bows *after* Hundley. Right? A fresh slate, Lois. Don't we sometimes get a do-over? Don't we?"

"That's one way to look at it, for sure."

"It's the *only* way," Clara said importantly. Lois remembered being her age. Momentous decisions rolled around every corner, it seemed, each day more tragic than the last. And boyfriends came and went. She was glad she wasn't young anymore.

"We'd better get out on the floor before Hank thinks we've abandoned him," she said.

They walked into the dining room, where a family of six sat at one of Lois's tables. Families didn't tip as well as the truckers who made up most of the diner traffic, but you never knew. People could surprise you. Lois glanced at her new shoes, at the little black bows. Love, indeed.

She grabbed an armful of menus and glanced at Hank behind the register. He wore a light gray blazer with charcoal shade lapels over a light blue shirt instead of his usual smock and apron. He looked sharp. Managerial. Better than she'd ever seen him. She wondered what it was all about. She looked again, closer, and thought her little black bows matched up nicely with his charcoal lapels. She was having a moment.

A glass shattered on the floor, and Lois swiveled to see a shaking Clara staring at the scattered shards. She ran over, gingerly pried the tray from Clara's grasp and put it on the table.

"Now, now, baby," Lois said as she slipped an arm around Clara's shoulder and steered her away from the table. Clara cried, letting her head loll onto Lois's shoulder as Hank marched toward the table with a broom.

When they got back to the ladies' room, Clara threw up in a stall. Lois waited patiently, looking down at the little black bows. When Clara finally came out, she washed her mouth and splashed water on her face, while Lois rubbed her shoulders.

"Now, tell Lois all about it," she said to Clara's pale face in the mirror.

"I'm pregnant. Knocked up. End of story."

She sighed. "And that boy—Tony—isn't coming back?"

"No, he ain't. I'm all alone, and my parents will kill me."

"You aren't alone. I'm here now. Hank will understand, too."

"Hank knows."

"Really?"

"You weren't around. I had nobody to turn to. He's been good to me."

"Well, that's okay," Lois said. There was more to Hank than she'd given him credit for. "You did right to tell him, hun."

"Hank said he'd do what he can to help." Her mouth quivered. "Bless his heart for being such a good man."

Lois studied Clara's face as the color came back into it. "Have you made a decision, with Hank's help?"

The girl looked away. "Hank said he'd pay for it. I don't have any money."

"An abortion."

Clara looked back at Lois. "It's such an ugly word, really. But I'm not ready to be a mother. There's no father to come around with presents and love. My parents would disown me."

Lois knew she was right. It was the correct thing to do, the practical thing. But the notion made her wince. She'd never been married or had kids of her own, and probably never would. At forty-seven, she'd missed that train.

"You've really made up your mind, hun?"

Clara whimpered like a puppy. "Will you take me, Lois? Will you go to Chicago with me to do it? I want to be far away from here to do it, but I couldn't bear to go alone."

Lois nodded and hugged her. "Yes, of course I will. I'll be with you the whole time."

Clara threw herself into Lois. After a moment, there was a soft knock at the door. Hank peeked in timidly. The hallway light made his forehead shine.

"Everything okay?" he whispered.

Lois stared at him for a long, awkward moment, seeing him clearly for the first time as Clara sobbed on her shoulder. "It will be," she said.

Fallen Stars

There was nothing to see, only lonely pinpricks of light marking distant farmhouses, as the train slithered along in the night. Their car rocked gently, rhythmically, and Lois decided she liked trains very much. She'd gotten used to the blaring horn, a sound that made it seem like the train was alive and lonely and calling out in the night, hoping for a reply.

Clara was quiet when they boarded the return train from Chicago. She shuffled along and then shrunk into the seat, with her head wedged against the window. Lois handed the tickets to the porter. He paused to look at Clara, who stared into the night, coiled tightly like a spring.

When Lois realized the girl had fallen asleep, she made her way back to the club car. She bought whiskey on ice and a Coke. She'd earned a drink after the day they'd had. Back in her seat, she leaned back and sipped. Soon, they entered a town. Light filled the car, and Clara stirred back to life. Lois gently rubbed her shoulder as she accepted the Coke.

"What are you drinking?" Clara said.

"Whiskey." Lois held up the glass in salute.

"Well, you've earned it, for sure."

"Why's that?"

"I was a mess at the clinic. I didn't mean to sound like a crybaby."

Lois mulled it over. "Well, no more than anybody else in your shoes, hun."

Clara crossed her arms and sank into her seat. "Now it's done with, I suppose."

"Time to go forward," Lois said, patting her hand.

"I know that. I made my choice. I'll live with it."

The train pulled away slowly, haltingly, and all the bright light from the platform fell away, leaving only a soft glow from the interior car lights as the dark landscape rolled in again. Soon, farmhouse lights glistened, like fallen stars.

"I didn't know they had whiskey on trains," Clara said.

"Sandwiches, too. But nothing to write home about."

"Nothing as good as Hank's meatloaf?"

Lois nodded. She wondered how he would manage with both servers gone for a day. Well, Hank had been okay with it because there wouldn't be much dinner traffic on a weekday. Hank was adaptable. One of his great qualities, along with generosity. He didn't owe Clara this kind of help, but he was doing it anyway. Lois reckoned that somehow, it meant the three of them were family; none of them had real family of their own.

"Well, now, Hank does whip up a mean meatloaf," she said. "Got to give him that."

"The melted cheese is a nice touch, like with lasagna. Where'd he learn to cook like that?"

"The Army." Lois finished her whiskey. The edge had finally come off the day.

"Why didn't you bring me a whiskey, too?" Clara said suddenly.

It was a good question. The poor girl had certainly gone through the ringer. She was twenty-two, and Lois should stop thinking of her as a girl. What she'd experienced made Clara a grown woman like few things could.

"I'll go get us one," Lois said, "or even two. How about that?"

Clara's face brightened. "It's like a girls' night out."

"Well, almost, hun."

"How should I have my whiskey?"

"You want it with ice, don't you?"

"Yeah, with ice. Lots of it."

"Then ice it is. Coming right up."

Lois came back from the club car, juggling a whiskey in each hand. Several times, she had to catch her balance as the cars swayed. She'd bought two more tiny bottles of whiskey, Canadian Club, for good measure. The young bartender had winked at her. She managed to plop down into her seat without spilling a drop.

"We have to toast something," Clara said, holding her drink up.

"It's your toast, hun."

Clara scrunched her face up to concentrate. "To Hank," she finally said. "After all, he paid for this trip. For everything."

"You should—by God—bill that damn boy," Lois said. "If you could find him, that is. He ought to pay Hank back for what was *his* proper responsibility."

"You're right. I know that. But he doesn't exist anymore. I don't let him exist, and so he doesn't."

Lois nodded but knew it was a false bravado. Things were never that simple.

Clara took a healthy sip of whiskey and made a face. "That's strong stuff."

"Once the ice melts some more, it will smooth out."

Clara drank again. "Wooo," she said. "It burns."

"That's what we pay for, the burn."

She sipped more.

"Slow down, hun," Lois said. "Not too much at a time. Rome wasn't built in a day. There's plenty of time to drink it."

"How long before we get home?"

"A couple hours yet. Might as well settle in."

"I'll probably fall asleep again, after all this whiskey."

"That's really what it's for, I guess," Lois said.

They sipped their drinks quietly as the train passed through another town. Light poured in on them from the platform. A girl about Clara's age got on and sat across the aisle ahead of them. She looked tired and sighed heavily, pulling up her hair in a bunch and then letting it fall onto her shoulders as the train lurched forward.

"I wonder what *her* story is," Clara said.

Lois hoped that whatever it was, it was different than Clara's story. *Better* than Clara's story. But then, Clara now had time to get it all into perspective. Dodging a bullet meant getting a chance to do something better. That was how to look at it. The only way.

"Maybe she's going to visit her grandparents somewhere," Lois said. "Out here in farm country."

Clara sniffed and frowned. "My grandparents wouldn't have anything to do with me if they knew where I've been and what I've done."

Lois placed her hand over Clara's. "No use beating yourself up over this, honey?"

Clara wiped a tear streaming down her cheek.

"We need more whiskey," Lois said, pulling the other bottles from a pocket. She filled their cups; the ice had mostly melted. They sipped and grinned at each other.

"My head's spinning a little, Clara said, giggling. The whiskey warmed Lois up. She was lost for a moment among floating, random thoughts, and she closed her eyes. None of the thoughts made much sense. In one of them, she was on a table, and men and women in white coats were doing something to her. She tried to stop them. She pleaded with them. Then all that vanished. When she opened her eyes, she wasn't sure how much time had passed. Clara was asleep, her head against the window. Hair drooped across her eyes. The poor girl had finally been worn out into temporary oblivion.

They were in a long, slow curve now, the train lurching like a rocking chair, or a baby's cradle. Lois could see a town ahead, a soft glow. They still had a way to go before home. Clara's drink was half-full, but she didn't need it anymore. Lois tossed it down and looked around the car. Passengers dozed off, read books, or chatted. Some frowned. Many smiled at each other.

A woman across the aisle stood up to stretch her legs and arch her back. Beside her in the aisle seat, a child woke and squealed happily. Lois asked if she could hold the child. The mother looked skeptical at first, but Lois's smile won her over, and she handed the girl over.

"You're lucky," Lois cooed as she rocked the girl in her arms. "So very lucky indeed."

Night Hawks

Hank locked the diner door, closed his eyes, and pressed an icy Old Milwaukee against his forehead. The long sigh seeping out of him had built up all night. He'd had to be a one-man band, cooking *and* serving, and for once, he was glad there wasn't much business. Hank now knew what it was like when Clara and Lois said their dogs were barking. Customers asked where they'd gone off to, and he'd shrugged and smiled and said they had the night off.

"Then do I have to tip *you?*" Old Man Farley had said. "I mean, you *own* the joint, Hank."

"Let your conscience be your guide."

"Yeah? Well, what if I don't *have* a conscience?"

"Then it won't matter, and you'll sleep like a baby, right?"

"You're using psychology on me."

"I don't think psychology applies to you, Farley."

Farley smiled. "I don't know what that means, but it sounds awfully clever, if you ask me."

"I wasn't asking you." But Hank smiled to let him know it was all fun and games, a long-running routine between them, small town ball-busting. Farley, who'd gotten rich from inherited farmland, peeled a few bills from his roll and dropped them onto the table. "For Lois," he said.

"I'll see to it."

He peeled off another bill. "And for that little Clara, too. She's only a baby."

"Kind of you."

But the reference to a baby made Hank wince, and he held the frown too long. He thought of Lois managing Clara down in Chicago. He glanced at his watch. They were due back soon.

"You okay, Hank? You look a little green around the gills."

"My gills are fine. I need off my feet for a spell."

"I reckon now you appreciate what a good waitress does, eh?"

"I always have, thank you," Hank said.

Farley was the last one out, and Hank sunk into his seat by the window. He slipped off his shoes and leaned down and rubbed his feet.

His dogs weren't only barking—they howled and moaned, too. He felt a burn up from toes—even his *knees* were sore. But he was also proud he'd gotten through it. It was the feeling of a race run well.

He sipped beer and glanced at the new picture he'd put up behind the register: a replica of *Nighthawks* by Edward Hopper. It could be like in the painting at Hank's Diner sometimes; during the week, a few solitary souls might haunt booths, drinking coffee endlessly, ordering fries or apple pie before trudging into the night to someplace they'd been putting off.

Night Hawks.

Hank reckoned he was a night hawk, too. Night creatures or nightcrawlers, as Lois and Clara preferred to put it. They hadn't known anything about the famous painting. It was only some old picture to them. But Hank had seen the original at the museum down in Chicago.

Clara had suggested the joint needed new pictures. Some plants, too. Those were next on his list. He'd pay Clara to handle that—it was a way to help her out—and she'd probably do a better job of picking pictures. He glanced at his watch. The last train from Chicago would arrive soon. He'd hear the horn soon enough; at night, you could hear it well before it reached the station. He wondered how they were doing now, how Clara had handled it all. She'd be all wrung out, for sure, but Lois would help her. She could do that. Lois could keep her head about her.

It was all a damned mess, but he immediately shooed away the image of blood and shook his head. That wasn't right, to think of it like that. That was ugly. He let his head fall into his hands. He wanted to stop thinking for a minute or two.

He raised his head and leaned back in his chair, tossing down the rest of his Old Milwaukee. He was mixed up in the thing now. No going back. It wasn't something that could ever get out. This wasn't Chicago. A thing like that could eat you alive in a small town. A regular customer, something of a busybody, mentioned to Hank that both his servers were missing, even though Hank explained that he'd given them time off. Farley could be counted on to remark that it was peculiar to see old Hank waiting tables and collecting tips. People would nod. Tongues would wag. Where there's smoke, there surely must be some fire. A rumor was all some folks needed.

If it ever got out that Hank gave Clara the money— No, that could not get out. It wouldn't matter about the damn boy who couldn't keep his pecker in his pants and then skipped town—some would see Hank's help as a sort of guilt. It could hurt business at the diner or damage Clara further. No, he would tuck away this secret for good.

He could count on Lois. But Clara—you never knew about young people until a fire started. But he wanted to believe she knew the drill. She wanted a life preserver thrown her way. She wasn't a bad girl at all— but not lucky so far. With a do-over, she might find her stride.

But some tongue-wagger—someone like old Farley—might ask, why the fuck put yourself out like that, Hank old buddy? Can you tell me that? Why risk putting your head on a chopping block? Even if that damn boy were to come back and own what he'd done, folks would still know Hank was the one who paid to get it fixed, although no relation to that Clara. Some might ask—why?

He looked up at the *Nighthawks* painting. Clara's dilemma was the sort of question people grappled with at times like in that painting, late at night, the day heavy on shoulders, with only a few people around carrying similar burdens. Maybe that was the best time to ponder a dilemma. He wasn't sure. He only knew the solitary man in the painting—the one with his back showing, hunched over the counter with his hat still on—that was him. Alone.

But he had Lois and Clara; they all had each other. They were like family, a family of nighthawks. In the end, paying to help Clara was an easy decision. You did the hard things for your family, despite any risks.

He wouldn't abandon them. His wife had run out on him, but he drew the line at betrayal. But life itself was surely a risk; that much was simple.

He glanced at his watch. A minute later, he heard the train's lonely horn in the night. *Here we go.* He had enough time to splash water on his face and sort himself out. Then he'd walk over to the station and see them off the train. He knew it was an important job, giving them something to come back to; it would make all the difference to see him standing there on the platform. They'd be at the end of their ropes, ready to hand themselves over to somebody else for a while. He'd walk them to his apartment and get them settled in.

And he'd cover for them at the diner if that's what was needed. He'd soak his feet in warm water—he'd ask Lois and Clara for tips on that. He'd always heard Epsom salts were good for feet. He didn't know what Epsom was. He'd ask Lois. They'd all draw in close together and work things out.

Night hawks survived.

On his way to the train station, he thought about the man in the painting. What or who was he worrying about? How many steps would it take him that night to find rest?

Hank climbed the stairs up to the platform and waited. The train horn sounded again, closer—louder. It was insistent, demanding, almost arrogant in the way it intruded into the quiet. He could see the engine's front light shining boldly ahead as the train leaned through the last curve before the station.

He accepted that he was a nighthawk, and at some point in the night, all he could do was wait for what the light of day would bring.

Blue-Eyed Girl

Walking to the diner, Tyler suddenly thought again about Afghanistan -- he couldn't see the method, only the madness. The destruction and violence. Team leaders had explained what it was all about, but to him, it still came down to violence without a clear purpose. Violence in the name of slogans and euphemisms. Blind patriotism. He never understood why they were there at all. Sure—911. He understood—historically—that part of the equation.

But by the time he reached Afghanistan, 911 was a distant memory. History. Nearly twenty years in the past. He hadn't grown up with 911; it was not his Pearl Harbor. As a kid, baseball had been his passion. It made sense to him, that wonderful game, when politics did not. The baseball diamonds at his high school and the park were refuges. Safe places.

He'd admire the clarity of the long, white lines between bases, and the lush, green grass in the outfield, where he was a reliable left fielder. The cheers from the stands washed over him like waves of pleasure. If someone mentioned 911 in school, for example, he had hazy notions about what it meant. But baseball was pure pleasure, the one thing that made him smile and feel loose and free. Baseball flowed through him as the fuel moving his blood.

He loved the smell of his Rawlings fielder's glove and often would put it over his nose and mouth and inhale the leathery fragrance, letting it fill his nostrils. He loved to smack his balled fist into the glove's webbing as he watched the batter awaiting a pitch. The crack of the ball off a bat was a heavenly sound. Electrified, he'd rush forward, judging where to make the catch. He didn't have to think when playing baseball. He was like a wild animal surviving on instinct.

After high school, Tyler would have liked to play baseball at a community college, but no college coaches had sniffed around to make an offer or encourage him to walk on and earn a scholarship. He finally accepted that his love for the game far outdistanced his ability. He'd only joined the Army because he didn't know what else to do. One day, a tall and lean Army recruiter in a crisp uniform with many medals on his breast came to his school and gave an upbeat talk about honor and patriotism. He handed out colorful brochures that made recruits seem happy and committed, strong and purposeful. Tyler asked about the food, and the recruiter said it was the "best chow in the best Army in the world. It puts meat on the bones, son."

Tyler nodded and signed up. He wasn't propelled by a great cause except to eat decent food and to belong someplace for a while until he figured out where to belong for good.

He still had the battered Rawlings glove in his footlocker in his rooms above Hank's Diner. He took it out sometimes to inhale the past. The memories were fleeting but sweet. When he slipped it onto his left hand, it already seemed smaller than he remembered from his playing days. Before closing the footlocker, he'd sneak a last glimpse at the glove nestled in a corner.

One day his platoon passed through the pitiful, crumbling village, and someone pointed out a blue-eyed girl wearing a hijab, sitting in a window. "That's what we're fighting for," the soldier said. "That's it wrapped up in a blue ribbon with a cherry on top, troop." But to Tyler, the girl looked annoyed at the group of foreign, uniformed strangers violating her village. She had seen much violence and destruction, had perhaps endured it firsthand or lost family to arrogant Americans who claimed to be there to help eliminate the Taliban before it made good on its plans for a repressive society. Tyler quickly became skeptical about whether they accomplished anything at all. Wherever they went, things tended to blow up. And the chow sucked, too.

The girl with blue eyes did not return his wave that day, and this event stuck with him throughout his entire tour. It felt unresolved and gnawed at him. He went home with it—the gnawing, the lack of closure. If the girl had only waved back, he could have walked away without needing to take her home, a pesky ghost to follow him around. If she'd waved back, he could have avoided the night hikes to avoid sleep. But blaming her was arrogant; this is something he was learning. She had nothing to wave about, nothing to feel good about. After some time, Tyler finally realized the girl did not owe him a wave. She owed him nothing. Probably, he owed *her*. An apology for tramping through her village, for strutting around Afghanistan like gods. For the violations of privacy. For the choppers overhead and the Humvees and the endless turmoil—and dust—they kicked up.

But that moment had come and gone in the flash of an eye, one day while trudging through a village in a line of dusty, tired, and scared men trying to make sense of why they were there. There was only constant change. Thinking there was any sense at all to make from tramping around Afghanistan, chasing an elusive enemy. One trooper from his platoon suggested the Army hadn't learned the lessons from Vietnam. You chased the Taliban in one direction, and they popped up in another. There was no premise at all, no black and white or clear right and wrong. It just *was*.

But now, Tyler was more at ease in the journey. Getting used to life after and taking pleasure where he might find it. He'd learned not to overthink life.

And on this night, he was hungry for some of Hank's special meatloaf slathered in ketchup and melted cheese, with fries to mop up the leftover sauce. And a cold Old Milwaukee to wash it down. He thought again of the blue-eyed girl. He wished her all the luck in the world and wondered how much—if any—he might have coming.

He'd resolved that when he was at the diner, or the VFW, or on a jobsite somewhere working for Mr. Rogers, if anyone asked him about Afghanistan, he would lie. He would tell them what they wanted to hear and no more. The slogans and euphemisms they'd heard before. Trying to make the war real to them was a mistake. They would not reward you for that but would prefer to palm you off with a "Thank you for your service." Most people would even tolerate if you were homeless and unemployed—as long as you didn't pitch a shitty little tent in *their* neighborhood.

But he wouldn't lie to himself. Lying to others was all right; most people couldn't stand to know how war really was. To most Americans, it was a video game. When people asked him about his time over there, they didn't really want to know the details. Details would only complicate matters. Inconvenient truths.

The war had recently and mercifully ended. Soon, nobody would ask about it anymore. Then, talking about it would sound like someone telling a ghost story that had lost its ability to frighten.

Shit happens.

And then you move on.

Scar Tissue

Clara had missed her shifts at the diner for three days, and Hank thought patience was one thing, but enough was enough. It was a slow Wednesday, mid-evening, and he told Lois he'd handle tables while she walked over to Clara's.

Lois had to knock several times, and when Clara came to the door, she looked like she'd recently woken up, although it was early evening. She wore yellow pajamas with pink and blue bunnies. There was a heavy dullness about her.

"Hun, are you going to let me in, or do we talk here on the stoop?"

"Hank sent you."

"I'd have come on my own anyway," Lois said.

"Really?"

"For sure, hun. Now, don't you think it's been long enough?"

"For what?" Clara said flatly.

"To come back to the living, girl."

"I'm not a *girl* anymore." She sagged against the door.

"That's right. You're a twenty-one-year-old *woman* wearing bunny pajamas. And here it isn't even seven o-clock at night."

Clara shrugged. "It is what it is."

"No, girl—it's disgraceful, is what it is."

"Stop calling me girl."

"I will—when you become a woman again."

Clara looked away.

Lois had decided it wouldn't do any good to try and babytalk to her. Some tough love was required.

"Don't pick on me—okay?"

"It looks like somebody has to."

"Yeah, well—that's my folks' job." Clara swung the door wide anyway and stepped aside as Lois brushed past her.

"Have you eaten anything?" Lois said.

"I had some Cap'n Crunch this morning."

"Girl—are you in the fourth grade again?"

Clara did cry and rubbed her eyes with both fists. She was barefoot, and her feet were dirty.

"Where are your shoes, girl? Don't you have little bunny shoes, too?"

"That's not right," Clara hissed. "You can't do me that way, goddamnit."

"Good. That's it—get mad. You *should* be mad."

Lois found a box of tissues on a table and handed her one. She looked around the living room while Clara dabbed her eyes. There was a large cross on the wall and several paintings of Jesus. A little manger set sat on the mantel, and next to it was a sign that proclaimed, "This is a God-fearing home." Lois had seen much of the same growing up before she escaped and put it behind her. She wondered if Clara had that ability, that strength.

Clara sat on the edge of a chair and looked up when Lois sat opposite her. "Why should I be mad?"

"Because you're better than this," Lois said.

"Am I?"

"Do you think you're the first woman to get knocked up and have to do something about it? Or the last, for God's sake?"

She whimpered like a whipped puppy. "Don't do this to me, Lois."

"You're doing it to yourself."

"What do you mean?"

"I mean you've got to snap out of it. You can't hide away in your little bunny PJs forever, eating Cap'n Crunch, for God's sake."

Clara coiled herself up tight in her chair, like she was willing herself to disappear. "Leave me be." Her eyes narrowed. "Why are you doing this?"

"Because I know this isn't you. It can't be, hun. I've seen how you can sidestep the grabby truckers at the diner and keep your cool."

"This ain't about some crude drunk trucker. How would *you* know who I am?"

Lois looked at the floor. When she looked up again, her eyes were moist. "Because I've been where you're at. Okay, hun?"

Clara uncoiled slowly, put feet on the floor, and leaned forward. "You never said. Not the whole time in Chicago."

"It wasn't about me."

"When?" she asked. "When did it happen to you?"

"A long time ago. A lifetime ago, really. When I was only a little older than you."

Clara rubbed her eyes and brushed errant bangs away from her face. "Jesus. I didn't know. I'm sorry."

Lois smiled thinly. "There's nothing to be sorry about. It's ancient history." She stopped herself from calculating the years in her head. She'd done her best to let it go. The memory was buried deep, an old wound encased in scar tissue. The memory hadn't bubbled to the surface in some time. But of course, the trip to Chicago with Clara had stirred things up.

"Did someone go with you, when you had it done?" Clara asked.

"No. I went alone."

"Why?"

"There wasn't anyone to go with."

"Jesus. I'm sorry."

"Why, dear? It's buried in the past now. That's how you have to look at it." Lois knew better than to believe that, but rehashing history wasn't going to help her put Clara into gear and get her solidly on her feet again.

"I don't know if I can ever look at it that way," Clara said.

"You will, hun. Trust me. Life moves on—and that's what you need to do right now. You need to find your get-up-and-go and get it going." She stood up and extended her hand.

"What's this?" Clara said.

"This is you moving on."

"Where?"

"Back to life. You're going to splash water on your face, fix your hair, and ditch those bunny PJs for your diner uniform."

"I'm not ready. "I can't go down there now."

"You can't afford *not* to. If you don't now, when will you? C'mon, Clara—chop, chop."

Clara stood awkwardly, and Lois steered her to the bathroom and hovered like a pesky butterfly as she changed and brushed her hair.

Okay, then. You look fit as a fiddle," Lois lied.

"I look a fright," Clara said. "The diner closes in a couple hours. What's the point of going?"

"Showing up. Being reliable. That's the point."

"Hank must really be mad at me."

"You know he's not that way. Anyway, we'll show him you're worth the trouble."

"If you say so."

"I *know* so."

When they got to the diner, the only customers were a pair of blue-haired older ladies in a booth. Hank smiled at Clara and handed her menus.

Clara blinked rapidly to clear misty eyes. "Thanks, Hank. For everything."

"Good to have you back."

Lois sat on a stool at the counter and watched Clara chat up the old ladies while Hank got a head start on dishes in the kitchen. Outside, the streetlight clicked on. Soon she heard the horn of a faraway train coming from Chicago. As Clara breezed by to give an order to Hank, she squeezed Lois's elbow. Lois closed her eyes for a moment and allowed history to bubble up again as she did the math. Her baby would now be twenty-four.

But it did no good to imagine a pretend life for someone who never really existed. She picked up silverware, rolled it into a napkin, and looked around to see what else needed to be done.

Crepes à la Lois

Hank locked the diner door, turned toward his apartment, then halted and froze. He mulled over Clara's abortion again. All evening, he'd managed to submerge it—enough, anyway—thanks to a better-than-usual crowd that had kept him hopping between the grill and fryers as Lois and Clara rushed from table to table.

Paying for Clara's abortion had made him the architect of the act—this was the sudden clarity that struck him. What if he hadn't volunteered? Lois and Clara would have scraped the money together for the trip and procedure. Clara hadn't asked or pressured him for the money. Maybe she'd been too proud to ask. If he was the architect, Lois was the chauffeur.

Weeks had passed, and Lois and Clara didn't bring it up anymore. Clara had offered to pay him back, but he'd waved that off. Her gesture even insulted him a little—although he wasn't entirely sure why. He wanted to believe he'd done something noble, but gestures were in the eye of the beholder. Plenty of the good townspeople wouldn't find it noble, and Clara's parents might hope for a cloud of locusts to carry him away. This image had worked on him some, the clustering locusts. He couldn't help but feel caught somewhere between *damned if you do* and *damned if you don't*.

Hank wasn't sure how damned he was. He wasn't religious, but he'd heard all the arguments and tended toward the side of practicality. It wasn't too damn practical, with her family situation, for Clara to become a mother. So, the matter got handled. He could have had more decisiveness during his marriage, should have fought harder for it. He did have that regret—he could have done more. He'd let her go too easily, he supposed. But water under the bridge was best left under the bridge and out of sight.

He started walking and found himself standing in front of the Amtrak station. Just like that, late at night. He'd always thought it amazing that he could walk a few blocks from his apartment, along a quiet street devoid of people, crickets in full symphony, board a train, and in a couple hours, find himself in bustling downtown Chicago riding a tsunami wave of strange faces, with the roar of city life almost unbearable.

Stars glittered above. Hank looked both ways, as if he needed permission to go on. His feet were heavy as anvils. But which direction? There was no one around to see him rooted in place, his feet planted in the cement. Soon, he heard the train whistle far down the tracks. The last train to Chicago. He could see the light peek around a far bend of the tracks, like it was shy to show itself. The horn sounded again, and Hank heard pride in the sound. That was an odd thought, but the horn made him smile. He'd heard it a million times and had always liked it. Maybe even loved it. It was the sound of possibilities.

He looked over his shoulder at the neon sign flashing Hank's. It was a fine diner. He'd made it that way. The food was good, filling—hearty Midwestern—and his two ladies made the service special. People liked Hank's. They didn't have many choices in town for a sit-down dinner with proper silverware, that was true, but they came to savor the homey aroma of the meatloaf, a cold beer, and the playful banter from Lois and Clara and sometimes, Hank, too.

The horn was louder now, the searing light from the engine an oncoming comet. Hank watched it, still stuck in place, mesmerized by the dancing light and insistent blare. The train to Chicago pulled up and sighed heavily, brakes squealing, hissing. Life glowed from it, infusing Hank, filling him with light.

An electrical charge hung in the air like a haze, filling his nostrils. He was virtually hypnotized by the train shuffling into place like he'd ambled along the sidewalk. He lurched forward, like the train soon would, his feet heavy at first. After a few steps, he felt light as a feather.

There was no right or wrong to it, only go or don't go. He would go with the clothes on his back and the money in his pocket—well, and a debit card. He would ride to Chicago, late at night, with no great plan or agenda, no timetable, because he could, and it would be an adventure. For a long time, he'd had too few of those. He stepped aboard.

Hank made his way to the club car and bought a cup of ice and two tiny bottles of Jim Beam. Slowly sipping whiskey and a leisurely train were made for each other. He emptied both bottles into the cup and sipped. Hardly a soul was aboard, only scattered passengers here and there.

He took a seat and looked out into the night, at lonely lights atop poles at farmhouses, at the occasional twin beams from a car hurtling down the road parallel to the tracks. He believed these sights were what Clara and Lois saw that evening when Lois was the good shepherd and Clara the lamb to be shorn. He had their eyes now, could see what they saw and hear what they heard. But now, with the darkness pressing down, there wasn't much to see.

He imagined Clara would have been consumed by fear on the way down. And guilt, lots of guilt. Lois, he knew, would hover close to keep her functioning. Lois had strength. She could stay calm.

Should he have escorted them? He couldn't decide about that and didn't think it had come up. He had handed over the cash and everything else to Lois. No, he decided, it was not a trip for him to have made. He'd done his part. He'd done *enough*.

But now he was running in their cold tracks and he felt it was good to at least have a sense of their journey, if not their actual experiences. That was enough, what he was doing. His little adventure. There was no role for him at the abortion clinic.

He was sure that was where Lois had shined. He would have been in the way there. He felt good knowing Lois had been there for Clara. He was seeing his longtime waitress differently now. She was someone worth having, and now, he had to admit he wanted her. He didn't know why it had taken so long to see that. But now it was clear.

He had a gulp of whiskey. It settled his mind, and he napped for a couple hours. When the train slid into Union Station, he felt fine despite the late hour. Once off the train, he swung by the McDonald's in the station for a Big Mac and fries.

Hank found a hard bench, which helped keep him awake, and when the sun began to rise, he finally went outside. He'd given Lois enough money for taxis, too; walking far would have been difficult for Clara. On the way there, it would have given her too much time to think, and on the way back, she might have felt poorly.

He walked east and crossed the river, lingering for a few minutes on the bridge to look down at the turgid water. Had Clara and Lois noticed the river at all? A small boat painted green with a bright red bow slipped along, and the young man piloting it toward the lake waved. Hank waved back and then walked to busy Michigan Avenue. The busy thoroughfare was waking up, and cars bumped along.

He had coffee at the Billy Goat Tavern and looked at the photos on the walls of famous people who'd dropped by. He found a photo of Frank Sinatra. Old Blue Eyes. Lois had blue eyes. He tossed down a shot of Beam for good measure, and then went out and up a flight of stairs to the avenue.

He crossed the river again, walking north. But he was drifting, really; he stopped to look in the windows at Sak's and watched the legions of people marching to work by the Water Tower. He felt he may be the only one in the pulsating crowd who lacked a purposeful destination or plan, and he thought of the empty diner. The temporary freedom suited him. He was on the loose, like a tiger escaped from a zoo.

After he'd rested for a while on a bench, he ambled across Michigan Avenue and looked for a good place to eat. He'd developed quite an appetite. He relished being on the customer end of the industry and entered Bistro 49 when the name caught his eye. He ate Crepes Suzette because he'd never had it before.

When he asked what it was, the waiter told him the dish had a cognac flambé. He thought about concocting his own version back at the diner.

Why not? Crepes a la Hank. He enjoyed the crepes well enough, but the Big Mac had been more filling. He'd swing by McDonald's on the way back and grab a couple for the trip home.

On the way back to Union Station, the sky began to spit a misty rain, and Hank sheltered under an awning. He was across the street from The Berghoff restaurant on West Adams in the Loop, a place he'd always heard about, and he crossed over and went in, brushing specks of rain from his jacket shoulders. He'd read once that The Berghoff was more than a hundred years old. Hank's Diner could make no such claim. Not even close. But Hank's was still a damn good, small diner. He could make *that* claim. Running it gave him an identity that satisfied him. He liked Chicago, but he didn't *need* it.

Hank had inherited the diner from his uncle after his discharge. The Berghoff was traditional, old-world German cuisine, with German beers in ornate steins. A gilded setting. Hank's Diner was a long counter, a few tables, and booths with leather seats. Cheap Old Milwaukee was the house beer. Hank's Diner had authentic charm; the people who made it work gave it charm. The Berghof was a famous restaurant, but they were a dime a dozen.

He drank a beer at the bar. It was an intimidating place, but he was glad to have finally seen it. He was like a little league boy seeing a major league ballgame for the first time. A dizzying thrill. He had a second beer, something German and pricey he'd never heard of—Spaten—quite tasty.

Unexpectedly, he asked himself again why he'd paid for Clara's abortion. Going over it one more time might finally put the sordid matter to rest, allowing it to sink into history. This contemplation seemed to come up as abruptly as the clarion call of the train's horn, erupting, the question ringing loudly in his ears—why?

Abortions weren't cheap affairs, and Hank wasn't made of money. It was not his kid. Certainly, he felt sorry for Clara. But she was no daughter. Then he thought better of that—in a way, she was. Blood didn't have to determine family. Sometimes, the lack of shared blood made for better families, the kind of bond he experienced with Lois and Clara.

Keeping the diner going glued them together, he supposed. He needed them, and they didn't have many other opportunities to make money. The diner was not a gold mine, but it should bring a good price when that day rolled around. Was that day rolling closer? He'd know when it was time, and what to do after. Maybe move to Chicago and find a life there. With Lois? That was an unknown. A big one. He didn't know whether she'd cotton to the idea at all after her last experience with Chicago, with Hundley the prick. But it was a possibility, a big enough place for a fresh start. He would let the idea ferment in his head and see what happened. There was much yet to keep to himself. Timing was everything.

He was in time to board a train for home. He ate one of the Big Macs and saved the other for Clara, who he knew craved them. It would delight her to no end. There was no McDonald's in their town, and a Big Mac was a great delicacy to her. The Berghoff and Bistro 49 would have blown her mind. Lois's, too.

He didn't have anything for Lois. A Big Mac was not the right gift—that was kid stuff. Lois merited something more personal, more meaningful. He could invite her to Rossington's for a drink after work, and that might be enough. Or he could name the crepes for her—Crepes à la Lois. Yes, that would do the trick nicely.

Of course, he'd have to eventually think up a dish to name after Clara, too. A good excuse for a train excursion to Chicago and another adventure. He'd warmed up to the idea. He should take Lois soon, he realized. A trial run. Even if it meant closing the diner for a day or two. Could Clara, with some temporary help, run it while they were gone? He couldn't say for sure. But it was worth looking into. His outlook was changing. More things might be possible than he'd ever considered before. It was a little dizzying. That was the whiskey talking.

Hank napped all the way back home. He'd learned to sleep just about anywhere while in the Army. When the train rolled into town, he had enough time to shower before opening for dinner. He lingered under the hot stream as the room fogged up like a sauna. It bleached the grime off and cleansed his pores.

He shaved, slipped on a crisp fresh blue shirt, and his best navy blazer. The shower had given him a glow. He felt the blazer was a nice touch, if a little dressy for the diner. But Lois had complimented it before.

He opened the diner as Lois and Clara waltzed along the sidewalk, arm-in-arm, as Lois chirped about this and that, and Clara smiled. Sisters in arms. That seemed like a doable expression. Everything seemed restored to normal, all in its proper order.

Back in his office, Hank looked up the recipe for Crepes Suzette on Google and felt like he could pull it off. Why not? He'd put Crepes à la Lois on the menu and see if anyone ordered it. He sent Clara down to Rossington's to buy a bottle of cognac for the flambé part.

He was ready to be surprised, for something new.

Independence Day

The commotion began abruptly, several days before the Fourth of July holiday. At first, a few here and there in the distance. Pop, pop, pop. The noise would kick up, peter out, and come back again, reminding Tyler of Taliban assholes sniping from a hill at his armored Humvee. As he paced like a nervous cat, his two small rooms closed in on him, tightening slowly like a vise. At night, he used a loud fan to mask the fireworks noise, and he slept fitfully.

On the evening of July third, the blasts increased, and some were quite loud, like mortar rounds, or even an IED. Long bursts, like an AK firing, cut through the night. Tyler knew it was coming from bullshit sunshine patriots making proud statements about freedom and sacrifice from the safety of their back porches. Redneck bravado fueled by Budweiser. They didn't know what he knew about sacrifice. If they did, they'd think twice about playing at war. But they wouldn't care. They wanted to get drunk and make some noise.

It was too warm to shut the windows, even with the fan on, so he walked around the block to the diner where it was air-conditioned, and he could sip a cold beer at the counter. An icy Old Milwaukee sounded good. Maybe that blonde girl, Clara, would be working. He'd seen her a few times and thought she was pretty. He liked how the curly ends of her blond hair bounced as she floated and flitted from table to table like a butterfly.

Hank had told Tyler he figured to work the Fourth because he didn't care to sit around all day remembering his own service in the Gulf War. War stories were for suckers, he'd said, ancient history best kept in the dead past. Tyler knew that war stories too often tried to rationalize war. There was nothing rational about it. Rationalization was one of the first things the military taught you.

Tyler chose a counter stool with a clear line of sight to the door and noticed that Lois was working, not Clara. He was disappointed but reminded himself not to have expectations. He'd never really spoken to Clara. He didn't know if she even knew who he was. If she found out where he'd been, she'd think he was one of those looney-tunes vets who freaked out at the drop of a hat. Or maybe that was his overactive imagination, mixed with a case of nerves because he wanted to get to know her but wasn't sure how to go about it. He felt having a friend near his age—a girlfriend?—could ground him, help him focus on something besides his memories of the war, or even help them go away.

His feelings about her were vague. Nothing solid, only a hunch she might be open to something. Then again, he could be dead wrong. She'd been a couple of years behind him in school, and he hadn't known her well at all. He saw her a few times in hallways, books clutched to her chest like armor she needed to hide behind. He couldn't recall seeing her with other girls. Those were his memories of her. But he had to concede they might not be reliable. Hell, he could even be confusing her with someone else from those days. Since Crapghanistan, his high school years seemed like decades ago.

Hank set an Old Milwaukee on the counter and Tyler chugged a good amount of it right away. The cold made his forehead ache for a moment. The air conditioning in the diner hummed, and if there were firecrackers going off somewhere, he couldn't hear them. A lull in the action. It had been like that during the war—long, quiet periods of boredom abruptly punctuated by gunfire and explosions. Uncertainty and dread waiting for something worse.

He sipped his beer and leaned his elbows on the bar. Overhead, a swirling ceiling fan reminded him of the twirling blades of a helicopter.

"I'd have one with you, if I wasn't on duty," Hank said.

"You're the boss here, Hank. You can drink a beer when you want, can't you?"

"A boss has to set an example."

"I reckon so."

Hank smiled and mopped up a coffee spill on the counter. "You want something to eat?"

Tyler ordered a tuna melt and fries with melted cheese. He'd never had a tuna melt. He wasn't sure what kind of bread was good for one, and he went with a toasted bun. He was trying new things. Thinking outside the box. He'd been inside the box too long. The Army had seen to that. The Army was a box.

"And I'll have another Old Mill," he said. The food was beer's useful chaperone. When the second one came, he was mindful to sip and not chug. He didn't ever want to get on Hank's wrong side. He was beholden to him, for giving him a place to stay. There were rules that went with that. He didn't want to seem like a day drinker to anyone, even on a holiday. But he felt like drinking a few beers. Why not? It wasn't like he had a car to get in and crash. It was a few beers, not day drinking.

"How's the job going?" Hank said.

"It's going good."

"Old Rogers treating you okay these days?"

"I can't complain."

"And who'd listen if you did, right?"

"That's right."

Hank stood behind the counter with his head tilted. "Rogers is a fair man."

"Well, he does right by *me*."

"That's why I recommended you."

"I appreciate that," Tyler said, raising his beer in salute.

"But do right by *him*, Tyler. He's a good friend to have."

"I keep my head down and work. Don't worry."

"That's the ticket." Hank went into the kitchen for a few minutes and came back out wiping his hands on a cloth. He put another Old Mill in front of Tyler. "So, how do you like that woodworking Rogers has you doing?"

"I like it fine. I'm good with my hands."

"You're a natural carpenter."

"You think so?"

"You've got the eye for it. Those cabinets you put up in the kitchen are first-rate."

Tyler sipped his beer. "I like building things. I've seen enough torn down."

Hank arranged mustard and ketchup bottles along the counter. He added salt and pepper shakers and fresh napkin dispensers. He leaned over, eyeing the array and straightening the line. "It's too easy to tear things down," he said. "Destroying things ought to become the hardest thing we ever do, my friend."

"You think that will ever change?"

Hank looked around the room at the customers eating and laughing, then at Lois writing up an order, and then back at Tyler. "No, I reckon it never will."

"Sounds about right." Tyler shook his head.

Hank went to the end of the counter and poured coffee for a new customer, a fat trucker wearing a John Deere cap too small for his head.

In a few minutes, Lois brought his tuna melt on a toasted sesame bun with cheesy fries. She smiled sweetly. "Bon appétit, Tyler."

"How's Clara doing?" he asked, immediately looking down at the plate of food.

"She comes on at four, hun. Ask her yourself." She winked and went back to the kitchen.

"Maybe I will," he said to her departing back, then began to devour the food. Tuna melts were okay, he decided. Toasty and tasty. He waited until he had finished eating to ask Hank for another Old Mill.

When Hank came back with the cold beer, Tyler said, "You know, now that I'm gainfully employed, I can pay you some rent." He liked the sound of *gainfully employed*. He felt good about saying it out loud, like he was finally getting back on his feet and leaving the Army behind. Ancient history, like Hank said.

Hank nodded and looked off in the distance. "Well," he said. "Let's see how it goes."

"Okay by me."

Hank wiped down a section of the counter. "I appreciate the thought."

"I can square my debts."

"I know you can. But build up some cash, son. There'll be things you need. Stuff you'll want."

"I don't need much."

"That's how it was when I got out, too."

"Yeah? How'd that go?"

"I had the clothes on my back, and it seemed like enough. And at first, it was."

"Hear that, Hank."

"If you came home with all your skin, you felt rich."

"Then I'm rich as sin."

"Ten-four to that."

They shook hands, both with strong grips.

"Did you come straight back here when you got out?" Tyler asked.

"No, I was down in Chicago."

"How long?"

"A few months."

"Yeah? How'd you get by?"

"I stayed with an Army buddy."

"That's some town, Chicago," Tyler said.

"It's big all right. Fast."

"Why didn't you stay down there?"

Hank stopped wiping the counter.

"There was no real work, except in factories," he said. "Or retail. Nothing with a future. Honestly? I didn't look too hard. Spent some time in bars."

"The same here, too."

"Yeah, but Chicago is much more expensive," Hank said. "If you don't have money or connections down there, you're screwed. I ran out of my Army pay and came home.

Tyler nodded and finished his beer. Another sounded good but he waited. Waiting to order another one was evidence of control. He had a buzz and figured to cruise on it for a while. He felt good, like he had his shit wired tight.

Hank's Diner had filled up more. There were a few families, and a good number of truckers. Their rigs parked for the holiday, they'd eat their fill of spaghetti and meatloaf with melted cheese—Hank's daily special—and then go down to Rossington's to get good and drunk, to brag about fishing or hunting prowess and talk about patriotism and freedom.

Truckers and redneck townies mixed at Rossington's to play the jukebox and hear songs about patriotism and freedom by country singers who'd never served. The singers and the townies wore cowboy hats but had never been real cowboys. These same men in this small town would guzzle cheap Bud Light and act like war was some video game. If a veteran showed up, they might clap him—or her—on the back and give a weak thank you for service they didn't understand. It was the least they could do for a veteran, but they'd deluded themselves into believing it was somehow a grand gesture. Anyway, that was how he felt about Rossington's the one time he went there. It didn't feel right to him.

Tyler would avoid Rossington's. It was not the right holiday to go down there. If he went, he wouldn't be able to keep his mouth shut around the loose talk. He'd cross a boundary, and something bad would surely come of it. Hard feelings, a fight, maybe. Cops and even jail time. He didn't need any of that in his life.

After a while, he heard fireworks starting up again in the distance. Pop, pop, pop. He was able to brush off these mild irritations like a mosquito. He focused on watching the door for Clara; it was nearly four. Hank brought him another Old Mill.

He started thinking about what he might say to break the ice. Something clever. He could compliment her. She'd be wearing a uniform, and he didn't know how to compliment something like that. *Nice uniform?* No—that sounded dumb.

He was never clever around women and trying to be often backfired, and he came across as simply weird. Don't overthink it. Remember to smile. You can't go wrong if you smile. He knew women liked a charming smile.

He glanced at his watch. It was time. He kept an eye on the door and listened for the bell above it.

But in the end, Clara called in sick, and Lois was quickly overwhelmed when a surge of business came in for the evening meal.

Tyler looked around at the diner's growing chaos—it was like a sudden attack, and they needed reinforcements. He pitched in and helped take orders. He cleared away dishes and wiped down tables until Lois and Hank could manage it all again. He even took a turn in the kitchen, washing dishes. He told Hank it was a down payment on his rent, and the older man laughed and patted his shoulder. When business subsided, they chugged Old Mills together.

And when the sun was down, and the sunshine patriots had mostly shot their bolts, the fireworks petered out. A single pop broke the silence now and then. Tyler had weathered the barrage. He was finally able to go home, turn the fan on high, and sleep as best he could. That was the plan. It was only one night to get through.

Nothing at all, really.

The Way of Things

It had been two weeks since her abortion, the Fourth of July come and gone, and Clara knew it was past time to get her feet under her again. One foot in front of the other finishes the race, Lois would say. Clara would try to believe it, and that might make it true.

Hank had given Clara extra shifts at the diner, even though he really didn't need the help. Lois was diplomatic about the competition for tips. They'd figure it all out, she said. Clara didn't quite know what to say to her. She felt ungrateful for cutting into Lois's earnings, especially after the older woman had dropped everything to help her.

"Water under the bridge," Lois said as they filled the napkin holders.

A second wave of customers would appear soon, mostly truckers ready to get off the road for the night. The more genteel, early-dinner crowd had petered out.

"But I feel bad about it anyway," Clara said. "Honest to God, I do."

Lois rubbed her forehead and glanced at Hank counting money in the register. He looked sharp in a tweed blazer.

"It'll all even out, hun," Lois said. "That's the way of things."

"Hope for the best is what you're saying?"

Lois rolled silverware into a napkin. "Things have picked up here lately – hope that it does some more."

"I could get on down at Rossington's," Clara said.

"Cocktail waitress?"

"Or bartender."

"You ready for what comes with that?"

"Like what?"

"Like, greasy, grabby hands from townies and truckers."

Clara shrugged. "How are they any different down at Rossington's than here?"

"They're *drunker* down at Rossington's, for starters."

"I'm not some baby anymore."

"No, you sure aren't, hun. Not after what you went through. But you aren't ready for Rossington's, either. That place is a slaughterhouse."

"How do you mean?"

"I mean, Bobby Rossington is a little creep who expects all his gals to sleep with him. That's what I mean. You down for that?"

"Not if I could help it."

"He'd bounce you right out of there if you didn't. Then where would you be?"

"Back here, I suppose."

"Really? Can you be sure of that?"

Clara's face reddened, and she looked down at her shoes. "How do you know about Rossington's?"

Lois finished rolling silverware into napkins. "Because I worked over there once, that's how."

"When?"

"Before I came to work for Hank. Back when I was not much older than you."

Clara crossed arms over her chest. "And?"

Lois narrowed her eyes. "And what, Miss Clara?"

Clara looked over to make sure Hank was still at the register. "You know—Bobby Rossington."

"What about him?"

"Jesus. Did you?"

Lois frowned. "Keep your voice down." She grabbed Clara's hand and led her away from the counter. Hank was immersed in counting money.

"What's the big mystery?" Clara said. "I'm not some prude."

"There's no mystery. Okay? But you can't go around saying stuff like that. What if someone hears you?"

"*Did* you?"

Lois whispered, "Do you think I'd do that to keep a job?"

Clara glanced at Hank, who looked over the menu. "I don't know *what* to think anymore."

"You must not think too well of me."

Clara's eyebrows arched. "No, no, that's not it. That's not what I meant at all."

"Then have some faith, *Miss* Clara. And no—I did *not* do it with Bobby Rossington, thank you very much. What a disgusting thought!"

"Well, I didn't think so. That's not you."

"Well, it could end up being *you* if you go to work for that prick. Okay?"

"Rossington's has its issues. I get it."

"It's barely a step up from a titty bar."

"Do they even have those around here?"

"There's one over by Claremont."

"How do you know?" Clara said. "Have you been there?"

"Don't you hear the truckers talk about it? It's no secret."

"I try not to listen to them, except when they order."

"You have to listen to *everything*," Lois said. "That's how you learn the way the world works."

"Well, I've got a lot to learn."

"You've already had a hard lesson." Her eyes softened. "How are you feeling?"

Clara looked away, touching her stomach. "I guess I'm okay."

Lois squeezed Clara's arm. "Regrets can slowly eat you up, hun. They're like termites. You can't let them."

"I don't regret it."

"Maybe you've got some *what if*s rolling around in your head."

"I suppose I do."

"Well, that's natural, I suppose."

"Weren't you curious, when it happened to you?"

"No," Lois lied. "Curiosity killed the cat."

"But it's okay to wonder, isn't it?"

"As long as you don't keep reliving it. Sometimes, the past sometimes needs to be buried." She saw the regret in Clara, the anguish building in the corners of her eyes. "Let the past be."

The girl teared up but managed not to cry. She pulled a napkin from a holder and dabbed her eyes. "What *will* do me some good? Can you tell me that?"

"If I could, hun, I'd bottle it and sell it."

Clara sniffled. "I'd buy a gallon."

"Me, too," Lois said. "Lois's Magic Elixir. But it doesn't exist."

Hank came over and reached between them for a stack of menus. "Well, ladies—are we ready for the onslaught?" His voice was loud, booming.

Clara stiffened and went pale. She covered her face with her hands and whimpered. Hank reached out to console her, but she pulled away sharply and hurried through the door to the kitchen.

"Now what?" Hank said, throwing his hands up.

"I'll go," Lois said. "You give us a minute."

"I've given plenty of minutes, Lois."

"You have. But you can give her another one. It's Clara."

"Okay," he said. "Fine. I'll watch the front. See if you can get her into some kind of decent shape."

Lois went into the kitchen, but Clara had gone out to the back lot. The door was open. Outside, Lois looked around and finally saw Clara standing next to the railroad tracks. Too close to the rails. The Chicago train was still far down the line, its horn blaring, but Lois could see its front light growing larger and brighter. The sun was nearly down, and the sky had an eerie red cast to it.

"Come back, Clara."

Lois checked the train's progress. Its light was brighter all the time, searching along the tracks. A breeze came up and ruffled Clara's hair. Lois felt a chill despite the warm summer evening. She went over to Clara and clutched one of her hands—it was cold. She squeezed it several times. Clara finally squeezed back, faintly.

"Did you bring some of your magic elixir?" the girl asked.

"Sure. How much do you want, hun?"

"All you've got. Gallons."

"Well, you're in luck, then."

"Funny—I don't feel lucky."

The train horn blared again, a long burst. It was very loud.

"Now, that's where you're wrong, honey," Lois said, squeezing her hand again. "You have all the luck in the world."

Clara looked at her skeptically, pulling a strand of hair away from her face but the breeze blew it back. The train's front light was now like a small sun barreling toward them. Lois felt vibrations coming from the humming rails. Even the ground seemed to shimmy.

"Is that right?" Clara shouted, her eyes vacant. "Tell me why I'm so lucky."

The train bore down on them, growing louder by the moment.

"Because you're alive," Lois yelled over the approaching noise. "And you'll live a long life. It's not your time."

"But it was my baby's time?"

"Yes, hun. It surely was. And I'm sorry."

"Then why bother? Can you tell me *that*?"

Lois gripped Clara's hand harder. "We do it for the chance that tomorrow will be better than today. That's why we bother."

"What happens tomorrow?"

"Nobody knows, hun. But if you're here to *see* tomorrow, you have a chance to get lucky. How about that?"

The rails shook and the train's light momentarily blinded them. But Clara's grip on Lois's hand was suddenly strong.

They stepped back from the rails and Clara sagged into the older woman's arms. They looked up at the passing train, hair blowing back from their strained faces.

Pressed against a window, a young girl with dark curls watched them as the train sped by toward the next town.

As Ever

The retirement home on the edge of town was a lot like its occupants: a dull gray, perpetually smelling of antiseptic. Tyler sat outside on a bench, working up his nerve to face the odor and empty shell of his mother. He was tempted to walk over to the diner and drink an Old Mill instead. It was Saturday, and Clara might be working. But he'd made it this far, and he couldn't slink away like some coward who wouldn't face up to things.

He took a deep breath, let it seep out slowly like a tire going flat, and reluctantly went in, shoulders squared like he knew from the Army. He would think of the visit as another mission to survive. It was a hard business to walk down hallways and see little old ladies with blue hair and withered, faded men with dead eyes, all wasting away. At the front desk, a plump, bleached-blonde woman smiled pleasantly, and he did his best to return it.

"Come to see your ma?" she chirped.

"How's she doing today?"

"Oh, as ever," the woman said, not looking up as she scribbled something on a form.

He walked along a hallway with a glossy marble floor. He heard raised voices and looked into one of the rooms; a gaggle of nurses in white uniforms flocked around a bed, fussing over an old lady with an ashen face.

The lady didn't move, and one of the nurses, older than the others, stepped back, hands on hips, and said, "Well, that's that. But we'll get Dr. Harrison to come over and call it, of course."

One of the young nurses looked up at Tyler. She was shaky, her face pale. Perhaps she wasn't cut out for seeing death as a routine part of the job. He knew from Crapghanistan, you had to see your first dead body to truly know what you'd gotten yourself into.

A shout came from another room, and he stopped for a look: an old bald man, his face shrunken like an Egyptian mummy Tyler had seen in a documentary.

The man sat up in bed with some effort. "I know you," he said.

Tyler smiled, because he didn't know what to say. But something made him stay.

"Come on in, boy," the mummy man said.

Tyler sat in the chair by the bed. A water glass with a straw sat on a stand.

"How about a drink?" He handed over the glass.

When the old man was done, he sighed, burped, and smacked his lips. "Hits the spot," he said.

Tyler grinned and put the glass back on the stand. "What were you shouting about a little while ago?"

"Shouting? Who was shouting? I don't care for anybody shouting."

"I heard you," Tyler said. "What was that about?"

He arched his gray eyebrows. "I don't recall any shouting."

"Well, that's okay," Tyler said. "It happens to the best of us."

"What does?"

"Shouting."

The mummy man frowned.

"Was somebody shouting?"

"It was a few doors down, now that I think on it."

He nodded. "That would be old Waterson. He likes to raise his voice."

"A complainer, is he?"

"All the damn time. Nothing suits him."

"I've known a few like that. So—they treat you okay here?"

"Are you a doctor?" Tyler smiled.

"No, sorry. Do you want me to call someone?"

"For what?"

"I don't know. More water?"

Tyler checked the glass, but it was still half full. He held it up, but the mummy man shook his head.

"I'm Tyler. What's your name?"

The mummy man stared at him for a while. "What?" he finally said.

"Your name."

"Did I do something wrong, officer?"

"No, not at all. I asked for your name."

He narrowed his eyes. "Are you going to arrest me, officer?"

"I'm not a cop."

"Officer Tyler?"

"Never mind. I wanted to know your name. It's no big deal. Names are overrated."

"Evan," he finally said.

"Okay," Tyler said, grinning. "I'm glad to know you, Evan."

"Why are you here?"

Tyler sighed.

"To see my mother."

"She's here?"

"Yes. Down the hallway."

"Your mother?"

"Constance—but she's always gone by Connie."

"Why is she here?"

"Early onset dementia."

Tyler didn't know why he was using formal terminology. Mostly, he was having a conversation with a whacked stranger to delay seeing his whacked mother. He cringed at the word – whacked. It made him queasy. He vowed to never use it again, to try and not even think it. It was a word that might apply to him some day, too.

The old man squinted. "I don't know any Connie. Or Constance, neither."

"That's okay, Evan."

Tyler got up to go.

"Did you catch him, officer?"

"Who?"

"Waterson. He likes to shout, you know."

"I'll speak to him before I go."

"You do that."

"Of course." Tyler started for the door.

"Son?"

He looked back. "Yes, Evan?"

"Don't ever let them stick you in a joint like this."

The mummy man's eyes fluttered, and Tyler figured he was ready to sleep for a while. A mercy, probably. And then one day, the man would sleep and never come back. Maybe even today or tomorrow. Tyler hoped he might get a better ending, but nothing was guaranteed.

He found his mother in a wheelchair by a window in the common room. She stared out the glass as sparrows twittered along a low-hanging tree branch. Her beautiful and long, silky brown hair was now gray, dry, and brushed back; the split ends dusted her shoulders.

Tyler stood next to her for a moment and watched the birds flexing their wings and chattering.

"They're a lively bunch," he said, looking at his mother to see if he would get a response. No emotion showed on her face. He pulled a chair over and sat down. They watched the birds until one flew away abruptly.

"He must have someplace he needs to be," he said and touched her arm.

She tilted her head slightly toward him. "I like birds."

"Me, too, Mom."

"You do?"

"I like them fine."

"What's your favorite?" she said after a moment.

"Cardinals. Those bright red cardinals always make me smile."

"Doves are my favorite."

"I know. You always said you like the cooing sound they make."

"Did I?"

"Yeah, you did. You said doves bring peace."

"I did?"

"Yes, often. Don't you remember?"

She swiveled toward him and leaned closer, staring into his eyes. "You're Tyler."

"Yes, Mom." A tear streaked down his cheek.

She smiled.

"Are you late for school?"

"I've got some time."

"When's first bell, son?"

"Not for a while. It's early."

"Well, I made you lunch. Salami and cheese. Mayonnaise, too. Now don't you forget it this time."

"I won't." He dabbed his eyes with the back of a hand.

She looked at him, pulling strands of stringy gray hair away from her face. Bags of skin had piled up under her eyes. He remembered when she had been beautiful, her skin smooth, her blue eyes lively. Now they looked dead.

"I forget your name."

"That's okay, Mom. It's Tyler."

She nodded and stared out the window again. The sparrows were gone. A breeze had come up and the branch swayed in it. Tyler placed his hand over hers, which were cold. He wasn't sure how long he sat there holding her hand. A nurse showed up and said it was time for medication, and that his mother was ready for a nap.

Tyler leaned over and kissed her on the forehead, and she clutched his elbow.

"Don't be late for school," she said.

"I won't. There's still time before the first bell.

"You best scoot," she said.

He watched her until she was wheeled out of sight and then lingered by the window, not really looking at anything. Memories washed over him. Senior year of high school when he hit his one and only home run. His mother had been so proud and overcome with excitement that she had bounded from the stands to meet him as he crossed home plate as the grinning catcher and umpire stepped aside for her. After the game, she took him to Dog 'N Suds and bought him a gallon of creamy root beer and two coney dogs with extra relish.

Slowly, he walked out of his mother's room and down the hallway.

At the mummy man's door, he looked in. The blanket was pulled up to his chin, and the old man stared at the ceiling.

Tyler went to the front desk to sign out.

"What's up with that Mr. Waterson?" he asked the woman as he signed his name.

"Waterson?" she said. "I don't believe we have a Mr. Waterson."

"Did you used to?"

"No, I don't think so. It doesn't ring a bell at all."

Tyler nodded. "I must have been thinking of someone else."

"Do you want me to check for you?"

"No, never mind."

"How was your mother?" the woman said.

"As ever."

Mousse

Hank shaved and stared in the mirror. He pivoted his head back and forth, assessing the gray flecks at each temple. They were subtle enough, and he was otherwise pleased with his hairline and t thick, dark hair he had on top. At fifty-two, he was reasonably sure he looked younger than his age. But handsome? He wasn't sure if he qualified.

Before opening the cafe, he checked his watch and walked across the street to Bert's Barber Shop. He told Bert to lightly snip the sides and top but to let the back grow more. He wasn't sure why. Bert looked surprised as he covered Hank with the smock. They stared at each other in the mirror for a few seconds.

"Going for the hippie look, are you, Hank?"

"Seriously? Where does *that* come from?"

"I said it, that's where. How's your hearing?"

"My hearing's fine. And there aren't any hippies anymore."

"You aiming to revive the tribe?"

Hank frowned in the mirror. "Why are we talking about hippies?"

Bert shrugged. "*You* kind of brought it up, Hank, with this progressive new hairstyle you're going for."

"I'm not *going* for anything. Can't a man let his hair grow without it becoming the talk of the town?"

"No need to snap at me."

"I wasn't snapping."

"Sounded like snapping to me."

Hank sighed. "Well, I didn't snap. I made an observation."

"Call it what you like. And it's your hair." Bert picked up a comb and scissors and studied the back of Hank's head. "You've got a lot of hair for a man your age."

"Is that a problem?"

"It's a plus for my business."

"Hallelujah, Bert."

"You know, plenty of men your age are already bald. That's lost business for me."

"Bummer, Bert. You should stock Rogaine—you know, to grow new customers."

Bert snipped a lock of hair and smirked. "Somebody woke up on the wrong side of the bunk, I reckon."

"I sleep in a real bed. Not a bunk."

"It's an expression."

"Yeah, well, we aren't in the Army, and you're not here to give me a buzz cut."

"The buzz cut is popular these days. With high school boys, mostly."

"Skinheads."

"I don't call them that."

"What do you call them?"

"High school boys."

"Whatever."

Bert stepped back and surveyed Hank's head. "How much do you want me to leave in the back, Mr. Hippie?"

"All of it. And don't call me that."

"You get a bad oyster or something this morning?"

Hank glanced at his watch. "It's not morning anymore. And nobody eats oysters for breakfast."

"That's just an expression."

"You're full of expressions."

"And what are *you* full of today?"

Hank looked up. In the mirror, he looked confused, a little angry. It didn't look like the face he'd seen that morning at home. What had changed? He paused while shaving that morning—suddenly quit, dropped his hands, and stared at his half-lathered face.

He wondered if a midlife crisis had snuck up on him. But he didn't think he was the type for that. It was something else. Something good, but also scary. It was Lois. He'd become fussier about his looks, about how women saw him. He wondered how *Lois* looked at him, and what she saw when she did. He now understood he had feelings for her, had realized this fact when he was in Chicago, despite telling himself for years to never get involved with employees But Lois was more than an employee. Thinking of her both thrilled and frightened him.

"Damn it, Bert— I should apologize for being so—"

"Prickly?"

Hank frowned. "Yeah, prickly about covers it. Sorry."

Bert looked in the mirror and smiled. "We all have our bad days."

"I shouldn't have brought it in here with me."

"Well, you have to take it somewhere, Hank. It might as well be to an old friend."

Hank nodded and offered a hand. "Thanks, old friend."

They shook vigorously.

"Think nothing of it, Mr. Hippie."

Hank managed to smile. "I don't think I'll let it grow *that* long, Bert."

"Whatever floats your boat."

Hank wondered what exactly *did* float his boat. He thought about Lois again. She was a good-looking woman with a good sense about her.

Bert eyed what he'd snipped, then ran the comb through.

Hank ran through the tally and figured it was going on fifteen years that Bert had been cutting his hair. "Thanks for listening to me, Bert, and putting up with me."

"Well, barbers are a little like bartenders. Listening is part of the service, I reckon."

Hank nodded. "Maybe you should have become a priest."

"Is that another one of those observations?"

"Sorry. How does it look in the back?"

"It's still creeping over your collar." Bert swiveled him around and handed him a small mirror.

"Uh-huh," Hank said, eyeing it from different angles.

"What's the verdict?"

Hank hadn't had his hair this long since before he joined the Army right out of high school. He didn't care to try and explain why he liked it to Bert when he couldn't explain it to himself.

"It looks fine," he said. "Dandy."

"Hallelujah. We have a winner, folks."

"Well, that sounds better than hippie."

"How about a hippie winner?"

"How about—we're done here."

"That's a mercy. You want me to put anything in your hair?"

"Like what?"

"A little bit of mousse, for better control?"

Hank looked at him in the mirror. Bert arched his eyebrows.

"I think my control's doing fine," Hank said. "I'm not aware of any complaints. But thanks for asking."

A knock on the front window startled them. A face pressed close, and neither could make out who it was at first, until she backed away a few inches.

"Is that Lois Nyberg?" Bert said, with his hands on his hips. "By God, it *is* your faithful waitress."

"Server," Hank said. "They like to be called servers these days."

"I don't see how that's an improvement. But whatever floats their boats."

Lois smiled and waved.

Covered to his chin in a smock in a barber chair, Hank felt like somebody in a wheelchair. He felt—vulnerable. He suddenly wanted to wave back but had trouble getting his hands from under the smock.

"Come on in," Bert called, and Lois waved again and made for the door.

Hank frowned in the mirror.

"Now, Bert, there's really no need to discuss my haircut with Lois."

Bert smiled when Lois came in and gestured toward his other barber chair. "Sit yourself down and take a load off," Bert said. "I was wrangling with Hank here over the length of his hair."

"What did I tell you?"

Lois chuckled. "Giving you a hard time, is he, Bert?"

"He's been a bit squirrelly. More than usual."

"I know what you mean," she said.

"*Hello*," Hank said. "I can hear you. I'm sitting right here."

Lois stood behind Hank, hovering. In the mirror, it looked like their heads were connected, and she had no body. She stepped back.

"Looking kind of long here in the back," she said. "Throwing caution to the wind, are you?" She winked at Bert.

"He's going for that hippie look," Bert said, chuckling.

"There aren't any hippies anymore," Hank said. "How many times do I have to tell you?"

"Well now, if you let that hair grow there'll be at least one hippie around here," Bert said.

Lois laughed.

Bert pulled the smock off Hank, and strands of hair floated around him. Hank stood up and brushed the hair from his trousers. Some dignity was restored. He'd felt a bit like a child sandwiched between Lois and Bert, having to look up at them.

"We hear you," Lois said. "Loud and clear."

"Well, thank God for small miracles."

Hank paid Bert, who handed Lois a small tin of mousse.

"On the house, in case Mr. Hippie changes his mind."

"I'll work on him."

"Good luck with *that*," Hank said as they walked out.

"It's mousse," she said. "It won't make you effeminate, Hank."

"Effeminate? Good Lord. Where does that come from?"

"It's just an expression, Hank."

"Well, you can keep that one to yourself."

"Duly noted, captain."

Lois even tossed him a sloppy salute.

"Captain, my ass," Hank said, but he tacked on a smile and Lois grinned.

They crossed the street and entered the diner. They would open for business soon but had time to prepare. Lois got the front room in shape while Hank puttered about in the kitchen. As she came into the kitchen, Hank was gazing at himself in a small mirror on the wall.

"Looking for the gray?" she said.

"I don't mind it, really. You know—it makes me look distinguished."

"Keep telling yourself that."

"You don't think so?" he said.

"I'm messing with you. You've got a good head of hair, Hank Spencer. Give you that."

"For my age?"

"For any age."

He smiled in the mirror. It went a long way toward wiping out all of Bert's hippie bullshit.

She took the tin of mousse from her purse and opened it. "It smells good."

"Yeah? What does it smell like?"

"See for yourself."

She held it under his nose.

He sniffed cautiously. "Not bad, I guess."

"It reminds me of roses," she said.

"Yeah, I can see that. Roses."

"You okay with roses, Hank?"

"I'm perfectly fine with them."

Hank couldn't place the look on her face.

"Turn around, Hank."

"What?"

"Face the mirror."

"What's this?"

"Do it. Live a little."

"I live just fine."

"No, you don't. You really don't. Trust me."

"Well, I'll be the judge of that."

"No, today *I'll* be the judge of it."

"You're crazy, Lois."

"Turn around. Let yourself go for once."

He felt like he *had* to do it, but he also *wanted* to. Resistance was now impossible. Unthinkable. Futile. He was in the grip of something. He slowly faced the mirror.

Lois stepped close, and her breath was warm on his neck. He shivered. His pulse raced. Her fingers were in his hair, gentle and coated with a cool substance. Hank's eyes fluttered.

The room smelled like roses.

A Transitional Issue

Tyler instinctively ducked as he walked into Hank's Diner, and the annoying little bell tinkled above the door. For some reason, he'd become more aware of the bell. He had half a mind to ask Hank to disable it—or let him have the pleasure of doing it himself. Though he knew to expect it, the sound was always abrupt, startling, and insistent like the pop, pop, pop of fireworks he'd endured. He wanted to reach up and jerk the damn bell right off the wall.

He chose a stool at the far end of the counter with a clear view to the door. He'd accepted that somehow, he chose this seat because of his time in Afghanistan, but it wasn't something he felt he could explain. It would sound like paranoia, his need to be alert, with escape routes in view. Down at the VA in Chicago, they'd told him it was a "transitional issue." Eventually, he would adjust to sharp sounds, they said. He needed to be patient.

But when someone came in or left and that bell tinkled, Tyler winced.

Lois looked up from wiping the counter. "You want an Old Mill, hun?"

"Ten-four to that," Tyler said. "Hank around?"

"He went to the bank."

"Counting his millions?"

"Something like that."

He nodded, and she brought the Old Mill. He chugged half of it. Her eyebrows rose, but she didn't say anything. The cold beer made his forehead ache for a few seconds, but he liked that. A perverse pleasure.

Someone came in, and the bell tinkled.

"That damn bell always been there?" he asked.

"As far back as I can remember, hun."

"You think it's time to retire it?"

"I don't really hear the blessed thing after a while."

"Lucky you."

"Luck don't figure in it at all." She finished wiping the counter and put fresh napkin holders out. Tyler ordered a burger and fries. Lois moved a ketchup and mustard toward him.

"You figure Hank is coming back soon?" he asked.

"As soon as he loads up the wheelbarrow with his millions, hun."

"I ought to volunteer to help."

"Maybe we all should." She went back into the kitchen.

There were a few people in booths but nobody else at the long counter. Tyler glanced up at one of the swirling ceiling fans. The gentle *swishswishswish* from the blades was a pleasant sound, like the fan he turned on at night to help him sleep. It was a warm day outside, and the cool air settled over him.

Tyler drank a second Old Mill with his burger and fries and felt full. When a customer came in and the bell tinkled, it didn't seem as loud this time, not quite as startling. Muted, but still annoying. That was the beer's doing. He sighed. It was too soon to go home. The diner was cool, and his two rooms behind it didn't have air conditioning—only the fan he'd bought at Walgreens. He'd stay a little longer.

As he sipped a third Old Mill, he thought about pacing himself to buy more time at Hank's. If he wanted to get his load on properly, he could walk over to Rossington's. It was always meat-locker cold over there. But he didn't care much for the place. It was too cowboy-wannabe. Nothing but country on the jukebox. The only vets he knew from Rossington's were much older, and he had trouble relating to them. Vietnam generation. Usually, he'd leave after one beer.

Hank slipped onto a stool beside Tyler and patted him on the back. "How was work today?"

Tyler leaned back to look at the older man. "I installed windows and hung some doors for Mr. Rogers."

"Yeah? Where are you two working these days?"

"Out at the retirement home."

Hank nodded and patted Tyler's back again. "Your mom's out there, isn't that right?"

"Yeah, she is."

"Well, I'm sorry about that."

"It's okay."

"How is she?"

"She doesn't know me anymore. She doesn't know *anybody*."

"Well, that's a shame."

"It is what it is, I guess."

"She'd be proud of you."

"If she knew who I was."

Hank looked away. "In her heart, she probably still does."

"There's always hope, right?"

"Where would we be without it?"

"We'd be fucked."

Lois came out of the kitchen. Hank looked up at her, and they exchanged bright smiles.

Watching this exchange, Tyler had the feeling they shared something unsaid, or they had a closeness from working together so closely. Lois wiped her hands with a cloth and glanced at Hank before going to a booth to check on customers.

"How are those kitchen cabinets working out for you?" Tyler asked.

"You've got the carpenter's eye, my friend."

"A cabinet door—any door—has to seat just right, or it's no good."

"You'll get no argument from me."

Tyler swiveled on his stool to face Hank. "You know, I've been thinking—that front door of yours don't feel quite right."

Hank looked surprised and glanced at the front door. "It seems fine to me."

"Well, it's subtle. But it doesn't feel like it should."

"I guess you'd know better than me. You're the master carpenter. The best in town, I reckon."

"Well, it's a small town."

"Doesn't matter. Rogers says you're tops. He was here for dinner the other night."

"Oh, I don't know who's best. Rogers is damn good. He teaches me tricks of the trade. But I can fix your front door for you. No problem."

"I know you can. But I don't want to put you to the trouble."

"It's no trouble at all. A simple adjustment."

"You sure?"

"Absolutely. Your kitchen tools are all I'll need. It'll take a couple of minutes, really. I promise."

Tyler fetched what he needed from Hank's toolbox and pretended to work on the door. After a few minutes, he put a short stool from the kitchen under the doorway and climbed up. He unscrewed the housing holding the bell and took the damn thing down. He felt a surge of adrenalin doing it.

Hank came over. "How's it going? Are we shipshape?"

"Well, the door's good to go now. Nice and tight. But the wiring to the bell is going bad. It's no good at all. So, I took it down."

Hank looked up at him, hands on hips. "Okay. I never liked the damn thing anyway. It came with the joint."

Tyler took the stool back to the kitchen and went out the back door past the dumpster out by the railroad tracks. He looked around to make sure nobody was looking, then he threw the bell as hard as he could, like tossing a grenade in Afghanistan. It made one final, annoying sound as it struck a rail and bounced into the bushes.

It was no longer a "transitional issue."

On the way back through the kitchen, he passed Lois.

"Bad wiring indeed," she said, smirking. "Clever boy."

"No comment," he said, smiling. Tyler sat down again at the end of the counter. It was finally shaping up to be a decent day.

Lois brought him another Old Mill.

"On the house," she said.

Tyler sipped his beer. He reckoned he'd earned it. Business had picked up, and each time the door opened quietly, he raised his beer can in salute.

The Setup

It was late, and Hank's Diner would close in fifteen minutes. Lois had gone home earlier with sore ankles. Rain poured hard, drumming loudly on the roof and roaring down storm drains. Clara finished up with the last customers, a mother and two children hunkered over dessert, pumpkin pie drenched in Cool Whip. Hank counted the till. Business had improved after the early summer lull, and Clara saw it confirmed in Hank's smile and the wad of cash in his hand. He nodded to her. She'd hauled in decent tips for the night.

The door opened abruptly, and the fresh smell of rain drifted in as Tyler brushed the water from his hair, which had grown out since he'd returned from Afghanistan. Outside, torrents of rain pounded the pavement, sweeping away dust and grime.

Clara didn't know Tyler. Not formally, that is. But he'd been a presence all summer, lingering in the margins, in and out of focus. His was a name mentioned sometimes by Hank and Lois, who liked his straightforward manner.

The last customers shuffled to the door. Hank kept a spare umbrella by the register, and he gave it to the mother. After he locked the door, he watched through the window as she herded her family down the slick sidewalk, the umbrella mostly covering the children, who clung tightly to her. The mother's hair was already drenched and limp. She'd promised to bring the umbrella back.

Tyler smiled when Clara made eye contact. He glanced around, like he wasn't sure where he should sit. He looked to Hank for help.

"I'll get us a couple Old Mills," Hank said. He looked at Clara. "How about a beer? You've earned it. What a night."

"I won't say no," she said.

She sat at a table by the window, and after a few seconds, Tyler sat down opposite her. They traded nervous smiles.

Hank came back with the cold beers, and they sipped quietly. Thunder cracked, but it was far off and not getting closer. The rain had lessened some. A car pulled around the corner, and its headlights flooded the window.

Hank sighed and eased back against his chair. "It was a good night," he said.

"Yeah?" Tyler said. He looked like he wanted to say more but words wouldn't come out. He glanced at Clara, smiled, and then looked down at the can in his hand.

Hank raised his beer. "To young people."

They each took a drink.

"What does that mean, exactly?" Clara said after she'd lowered hers.

"I think he means us," Tyler said.

"Oh, I know that. But why?"

Hank shrugged, his hands cupping the beer. "Why not?"

"Okay—whatever. I didn't mean anything by it."

"Are you okay?" Hank said.

She shrugged and had a sip of beer. "Why wouldn't I be?" she said. "I like to know what I'm toasting. That's all."

"So, Hank," Tyler said. "Is tonight a sign of business to come?"

Clara laughed. Tyler and Hank exchanged curious looks.

"I'm sorry," she said, chuckling. "That—it sounded funny, how it came out. Very formal. Like a board of directors meeting."

Tyler frowned, and Clara thought he looked a bit like a scolded puppy.

"We'll do okay the rest of summer," Hank said.

"Do you like being a carpenter, Tyler?" she asked.

"I like working with my hands."

"Jesus was a carpenter, wasn't he?" she said.

"That's what they say. I've never read the Bible, though."

"Really?" She leaned forward. "Never?"

He shrugged. "It never really came up in my family."

"Not even when you were in Afghanistan?"

He mulled it over. "I don't think it would have helped much over there."

"Really?" she said. "Not at all?"

Tyler shrugged. "I never saw God in any of it. I don't think a merciful God would allow all that. But don't go by me."

"I wonder if there really is a God," she said. "My parents swear there is, of course."

"What do *you* think, Hank?" Tyler said.

"I think it's time I got us more beer." Hank stood up, stretching.

"I'll do it," Clara said.

In the kitchen, she looked at herself in a mirror and let her hair down. She pulled her long bangs back, and they fell onto her cheeks, framing her face nicely. It made her face seem thinner. Her blonde hair, she knew, was her best feature. She took the beers back and served Tyler first.

She raised her can. "What should we drink to *this* time?"

"I don't know," Hank said. "What do *you* think, Tyler?"

Tyler studied Clara's face. "To always telling it like it is," he said. "That's what we should drink to."

"I can buy that," Clara said after her sip. It was clearly a setup, this encounter with Tyler. But she decided to ride it out and see what it was about. She trusted Hank's judgment. He'd done right by her when she'd needed help.

"To the truth," Hank said, and they all drank again. He stood. "I have to attend to something in the kitchen."

"Well, that wasn't obvious," she said after he left.

"Hank's a good man," Tyler said.

"You live in that little apartment in the back of the building, right? How is that?"

"It's a place to sleep. It's okay."

"People always say things like that, but I wonder how true it is."

"I don't really need much," Tyler said. "It's a bed and a roof over my head."

"Do you think people worry too much about having things, Tyler?"

It was the first time she'd said his name, and it thrilled him.

"Yeah, I do. What do we really need, Clara, when it all comes down to it? Shelter, mostly."

He liked saying her name.

"I've never had much," she said. "My parents are average. *Below*, probably. They live by the Bible."

"And you?"

"Average, average, average," she said. "But somebody has to be, I suppose."

"There's nothing wrong with average," Tyler said. "Not everybody can be some sort of celebrity. I wouldn't want all the attention."

"How about the money? Would you want all the money?"

"I'm starting to make decent money now," he said. "I'll make more in the future. I'm not complaining."

"That's right," she said. "You're a carpenter. Like Jesus."

He grinned. "You like to pull people's legs, don't you?"

"It's my hobby. Don't you know that?"

He could tell she wasn't serious. He figured it was a defense mechanism. A shrink down at the VA had explained defense mechanisms, which sometimes came in handy. Rationalization was a defense mechanism the Army had taught him, one you needed big-time in a shithole like Afghanistan. But he was shedding it. He'd made progress with that.

"I do know," he said. "You like to throw up a roadblock to see if somebody can get around it. We all do that."

"Really?" she said. "That's an interesting theory. Did they teach you psychology in Afghanistan?"

"Yeah, the psychology of bullshit."

Images came back to him, swirling, but they were fleeting now. Shards of memories. They seemed less and less real. He knew that was a good thing. Progress. He no longer accepted rationalization. That dead end was not a road he traveled on anymore.

"I suppose I could use some psychology, too," she said.

"Oh, I don't know. Be honest with yourself and everybody else."

"Very profound, Dr. Tyler."

"But isn't it really common sense?"

She tucked some hair behind her ear and studied his face.

"What are we talking about here?"

She shrugged. "Life. How to live."

"That's a tough one all right."

"Sometimes I feel like I'm waiting for a train that never shows up," she said.

"Maybe find another train?" he said.

"Or stop looking for one altogether?"

Clara glanced out the window. The rain had stopped, and pools of water dotted the street, while the moon shone in their reflections. A car plowed through a pool and showered water on the sidewalk. She looked back at Tyler. He was a nice-looking boy—man—and he had a kind face. She liked how his hair had grown out.

"I had an abortion," she said.

"Oh," he said, nodding. "When was this?"

She started to calculate the days and weeks but decided it was finally irrelevant. "Earlier this summer," Clara said. "In Chicago. Lois took me down."

"I like Lois," he said.

"I couldn't have gotten through it without her."

"But you did, and now it's behind you. You survived."

"What does that mean, exactly?"

"It means exactly that—you *survived*. Life is about surviving. I've figured that much out at least."

Clara managed a weak smile. "I suppose you're right."

Tyler clasped his hands on the table. "I've killed people."

She nodded. She'd wondered about that. She should have been surprised but wasn't.

Slowly, she reached a hand across the table and grasped one of his. They sat like that, quietly, until Hank came out of the kitchen.

92

Heat Lightning

Lois swung her legs onto the floor and pulled her panties on. She sighed before pushing away from the bed.

Hank woke up, his hair a tangled mess. He rubbed his eyes. Lois went to the window and looked out at the low-lying, dark clouds. The town was socked in.

She slid open the window. "A hard rain's coming," she said. "I can smell it working up."

Hank sniffed and rubbed his eyes again, focusing. "You should be on the weather channel."

"That's funny. You could be a comedian."

"It probably pays better than running a diner."

"But only if you're actually funny."

"And good morning to you, too," he said, sitting up.

She looked out the window. "Can't you smell the rain?"

Hank got out of bed and pulled on his Levi's. "What does it smell like?"

"It smells fresh," she said. "Clean."

He went to the window and draped his arm around her. She sagged into him.

"How long before it rains, weather lady?"

"Any moment now."

"I see."

"Or not at all."

"Well, that's clear as mud."

"The front might move along after a while," she said. "Maybe it's not ready to rain yet."

Hank stuck his head out the window and looked up. "I don't know. It looks serious up there."

"It's teasing us," she said. "Or it could be a sign."

"Of what?"

"A sign of something bad."

"Well, that's not how farmers would see it."

"We're not farmers."

He squeezed her shoulder. "Or a sign of something *good.*"

"Maybe."

"Can we look at it *that* way?"

"Maybe."

"Have you heard thunder yet?" he said.

"No."

"How about lightning—seen any?"

"Not yet."

"Are you wishing for some?"

"I don't know. What's the difference between them?"

"Lightning is the flash and thunder is the sound."

"Then they're bound together," Lois said, smiling.

"One doesn't happen without the other," he said. "They're one and the same."

Hank looked up at the charcoal clouds. They were thick. Heavy. Dense. Even menacing. But he'd seen dark clouds come and go without a drop of rain, without a sound. A dark, meaningless mass drifting along until out of sight over the horizon. Nature being mysterious.

"I'll make us some coffee," he said.

"That's fine. I'm ready for it."

When he brought her a cup, she'd slipped on one of his dress shirts, a blue one.

"A breeze came up and I felt a chill," she said after a sip.

"But now you're fine?"

"I'm perfect, but I need a shower."

"The shirt suits you."

"I'll wear it when we go down and open the diner," Lois said, smiling.

He smirked. "What if I wear one just like it?"

"People will talk."

He grinned back. "Let them."

"About the shirt? Or other things, Hank?"

"All of it. That business with Clara, down in Chicago."

"The abortion."

He glanced down but quickly realized he should keep eye contact. "Yeah, we can say it out loud," he said. "We never really did, but now we should. It's not some dirty little secret."

She turned away. "Loss is part of life."

"And now Clara's had hers. I've had mine. But we're okay, Lois."

She faced hm again. She swiped at a tear with the back of her hand. "You didn't ask what *I* lost, Hank."

He felt like an actor who didn't know his line. "What did you lose, Lois?"

She sighed. "I had an abortion, too."

"Jesus, Lois. I had no idea."

He felt a little queasy.

"Nobody else knows," she said. "It's ancient history, really. But all that business with Clara brought it back to the surface."

He hesitated, but then recovered and pulled her close and tight and that was the only reply needed. He felt her wet cheek against his. They stayed like that a while, gently swaying together, like slow dancing. The embrace melted slowly, and Lois looked into his eyes, smiled bravely, and went to the bathroom.

Hank heard the shower come on. The steady flow of water was soothing. He sipped his coffee and sat beside the window, watching the clouds. He saw a flash but did not hear the bark of thunder. It was only heat lightning, the sign of a storm moving away.

Acknowledgements

Much thanks to my personal editor, Carol Burbank at Storyweaving, and to Mary Vensel White and Katie Schwab at Type Eighteen Books for their wise editing.

Thanks, as always, to Stuart Dybek, a major inspiration to me.

And thanks, still, after all these years, to the late Daniel Curley, the first real writer to tell me I had the right stuff, too.

And I want to mention two wonderful friends, Anthony Squiers and Katie Gantt, who are like family.

--Michael Loyd Gray

About the Author

Michael Loyd Gray is an invited member of the Society of Midland Authors and has published eight novels and fifty short stories. He earned an MFA from Western Michigan University, a bachelor's from the University of Illinois, and has taught at universities and colleges.

Gray's novel *Well Deserved* won the 2008 Sol Books Prose Series Prize, and *Not Famous Anymore* garnered a support grant from the Elizabeth George Foundation in 2009. His novel *Exile on Kalamazoo Street* was released in 2013. *The Canary,* which reveals the final days of Amelia Earhart, was released in 2011. *King Biscuit,* a Young Adult novel, was released in 2012. Gray is the winner of the 2005 *Alligator Juniper Fiction Prize* and 2005 *The Writers Place Award for Fiction*.

Gray lives in Kalamazoo, Michigan, where he collects electric guitars, roots for the Chicago Bears, and tries to keep up with two cats, Suzie Lucifer and Yoda Lucifer.